NEVER LET HER GO

"If there were ever a woman I decided to wed, it would be you."

She stared up at him, then began to laugh.

"I did not expect you to be amused by such a confession," he said.

"You should when you try so hard to sound noble. It does not suit you, Neville." She laughed again. "But that was a very fine speech, no matter how unwilling each word was."

He shook his head in amusement. When would he recall that Priscilla seldom reacted as other women did?

She walked to the bed and picked up one of the pillows, steadying herself so she did not knock herself off her feet with the slight motion. Raising the pillow, she said, "I believe it is time to make my aunt very happy."

"Me first." He hooked an arm around her waist and tugged her to him.

The pillow dropped to the floor as he captured her sweet lips. Her breath, swift and unsteady, filled his mouth as he tasted the luscious flavors within hers. Even as he savored holding her close, a small, taunting voice in his head was telling him he was a fool to leave this woman and the pleasure they could share. . . .

FAIRE GAME

JO ANN FERGUSON

ZEBRA BOOKS
Kensington Publishing Corp.
http://www.kensingtonbooks.com

ZEBRA BOOKS are published by

Kensington Publishing Corp.
850 Third Avenue
New York, NY 10022

All Kensington titles, imprints and distributed lines are available at special quantity discounts for bulk purchases for sales
promotion, premiums, fund-raising, educational or institu-
tional use.

Special book excerpts or customized printings can also be created to fit specific needs. For details, write or phone the office
of the Kensington Special Sales Manager: Kensington Publishing Corp., 850 Third Avenue, New York, NY 10022. Attn.
Special Sales Department. Phone: 1-800-221-2647.

First Printing: June 2003
10 9 8 7 6 5 4 3 2 1

Printed in the United States of America

For Gail Eastwood-Stokes
never forget all of our parking lot tours

PROLOGUE

It would be so simple. In another time and another place, it might be more complicated, but this time and place were perfect. With a clear head and a steady hand, it could not fail.

The field was empty, save for a single person dressed in an outfit and colors that brought Robin Hood to mind. The person bent to a canvas bag lying in the trampled grass and withdrew a slender item.

Running a finger along the arrow that had been notched to fit in a crossbow, the lone archer smiled. Long ago, these arrows had been called quarrels. This arrow might be the very one to start the quarrel that would end in success.

The archer picked up the bulky crossbow and knelt on one knee. With skill gained from much practice, the archer put one foot in the stirrup at the front of the bow and fit the quarrel beneath the string. The archer stood, and the arrow was caught by the notch connected to the trigger.

Smiling, the archer hefted the crossbow and sighted on the target. Soon, this meadow would be crowded, but now no one else faced the target. It leaned against a stack of hay. It would do for today. This was only practice.

The sunlight burning through the trees forced the archer to squint, but exactness was not necessary. The target would be waiting when the time was right.

Taking a deep breath and releasing it, the archer contracted the rudimentary trigger. The quarrel sliced the air with a vicious hum before striking the target with a sickening thump. It hit the center of the innermost circle.

The bowman leaned the crossbow across one shoulder and walked jauntily toward the target. Putting one foot against it, the archer pulled the arrow from its black heart. Bits of straw clung to the tip. It had driven deep into the bale of hay, as deep as the span of a man's body. Patting the crossbow, the archer smiled and glanced at the windows overlooking the meadow and glittering in the rising sun.

It would be simple . . . and just the beginning.

ONE

Some days, Lady Priscilla Flanders wanted to strangle Aunt Cordelia. Other days, she preferred the idea of boiling her father's sister in oil or stashing her away in an iron maiden. This afternoon, she was wondering if it would be possible in the seaside village of Stonehall-on-Sea to rent a coliseum, a bloodthirsty crowd, and a hungry lion.

Her aunt had arrived this morning at Mermaid Cottage, and already the whole household was on edge. It might have been because her aunt was horrified to find Priscilla's son, Isaac, at home instead of school. Even assuring her aunt that Isaac was on holiday for the Michaelmas quarter day had done nothing to soothe Aunt Cordelia.

"He is too often not at his studies," Aunt Cordelia said as she sat on a bench in Mermaid Cottage's garden. The last flowers of the season were boldly showing their fall colors in the basket she held on her lap, the golden chrysanthemums only a few shades brighter than her hair.

"He is diligent at school," Priscilla replied, as she had a half-dozen times since this conversation began. "A boy also needs to learn things not found in books."

"Mischief, you mean." Her frown revealed the

lines in her face that her aunt usually kept covered with rice powder. "What use does an earl have for such activities?"

Priscilla considered answering with the truth, because the tales that had come down through the family of previous earls of Emberson suggested Isaac's youthful mischief was far more innocent than some of their less-than-heroic deeds. To own the truth, the whole line was renowned for being reckless at times. Such an answer would not do for her aunt, who seemed to forget those stories when she took on this tone that suggested she—and she alone—knew what was best for the current earl. Aunt Cordelia must not be allowed to forget that the current earl would be celebrating only his tenth birthday in two months.

"He is on holiday, Aunt Cordelia," Priscilla replied as she finished repairing the hole in her son's breeches. Doing mending was a task she could have left to one of the maids, but Isaac went through breeches too quickly for the normal schedule for mending. She set the well-patched breeches on her lap. "And he is working on a project for his instructors at Langley Academy."

Her aunt sniffed, a sure sign that Aunt Cordelia had run out of arguments but was not ready to acquiesce.

Priscilla looked past her aunt toward the sea. It was visible beyond the stables at the far end of the garden. A thin line of clouds clung close to the horizon, and she guessed rain would be returning to help batter the slowly changing leaves to the ground.

She loved this comfortable house, which was more like home than the one on Bedford Square in London, so she had been happy to return here last month. Her garden was burgeoning with color, and she could enjoy a pleasant conversation with her neighbors on one side—the Muir brothers, elderly twins who were always together. The cottage on the other side of her garden was currently empty, a stark reminder of the troubles that had plagued the village in the spring. Now that cloud, unlike the ones edging the sea, was gone. She should be content.

But she was not. Since she and the children had returned to Mermaid Cottage, she had heard nothing from Neville. Not that she expected him to write. Such a pastime was too sedentary for a man like Sir Neville Hathaway, who had had varied careers from thespian to thieftaker before receiving his title and fortune from a distant uncle. Yet she missed his calls.

"Mama!"

Priscilla shoved aside her dreary thoughts as her middle child, Leah, burst from the house at a pace that earned a frown from both her mother and great-aunt. Neither expression seemed to discourage Leah, who ran to them. As always, Leah's hair was ajumble and the ribbons on her dress cockeyed. No amount of suggestions on how she should behave made any difference, and Priscilla secretly was delighted that her younger daughter took such excitement from life.

"Mama! You must come and see this!" Leah was almost jumping up and down in her excitement.

Priscilla stood. Putting her hand on her daughter's shoulder before Leah bounced into a flower bed, she said, "I will, but please calm yourself."

"How can I, Mama, when *that* is going by the house?"

"That what?"

Then she heard the unmistakable sound of many

wagon wheels. It was noise she was accustomed to in London, but not here. Traffic along the road paralleling the shore was infrequent because Stonehall-on-Sea was set on a tongue of land reaching out into the ocean, and most carriages and drays passed by it inland.

"Come and see." Leah grasped her hand and tugged.

Nodding, she went with her daughter through the house to the front door. She was not surprised to find it open and her other two children gathered on the steps. Both footmen stood there, too, and Gilbert, her butler, was looking over her son's head.

Priscilla understood why when she saw the brightly colored parade passing in front of the cottage. The wagons could have belonged to gypsies, but each one stated it belonged to the WANDERING MINSTREL THEATER TROUPE.

"Do you think they are going to stop in Stonehall-on-Sea?" asked Isaac as he tried to push past his sisters to see. "Can we go to the theater to celebrate Daphne's birthday next week?"

"I don't know the answer to your first question, so I cannot answer your second one," she replied.

A young man waved from one of the wagons, and she glanced at her oldest. Daphne would soon be old enough to be part of the Season, although not soon enough in her blond daughter's opinion. Her daughter was smiling shyly as she wagged her fingers in an almost imperceptible wave in return.

Priscilla heard her aunt gasp. Her own eyes widened when she saw a trio of women slip out of a bright blue wagon. They were completely covered from chin to toe in translucent fabric. They began to dance alongside the wagon.

"Children," Aunt Cordelia said, "do come inside. This is not a proper performance for you to view."

Shooing her children inside, Priscilla motioned for the mesmerized footmen to follow. They did, albeit slowly and with their necks stretching to catch every possible sight of the dancing women.

"What was that?" asked Aunt Cordelia as the children rushed up the stairs.

Knowing they were on their way to look out the front windows of the house, Priscilla started after them. She replied while climbing the steps. "I have no idea, but I intend to find out."

The door opening woke Priscilla. She wanted to hide her face back in the pillows and recapture the pleasant dream that was already disappearing. The day had been long, with a walk into Stonehall-on-Sea to discover if anyone knew if the theater troupe was stopping or just passing through the village. Everyone had been agog with the view of the garish wagons and the dancing women. Constable Forshaw had spoken with a man on the first wagon and was reassured that the troupe was not planning on staying in the village. They were bound for Stenborough Park, several miles from Stonehall-on-Sea, for a quarter-day gathering.

She was glad about that, especially after overhearing Mrs. Moore chiding the footmen for talking too much about the brazen dancing women. The housekeeper usually left such scolds to Gilbert, so she must have been very upset to intrude on the butler's duties.

The bed bounced, and Priscilla gasped.

"Mama, come and see!" she heard from beyond the bed curtains.

"Leah?" She blinked. The light from the candle her younger daughter held seemed more brilliant than the midday sun. "What is amiss? Did you have a bad dream?"

"No!" She leaned against the bed again, jarring it. "I was up to get a drink of water, and I saw it."

"It?" Priscilla took the candle from her daughter before wax dripped on the bed, lighting the lamp by her bedside and blowing out the candle.

"Something in the front garden." Leah's voice was high with excitement.

"Something?" She tried to make her groggy mind function. "An animal of some sort?"

"No, 'tis a tent."

"A what?" She swung her feet over the side of her bed. Picking up her wrapper, she stood. "Leah, why would there be a tent in our front garden?"

"I don't know, Mama, but it is there." Looking over her shoulder, she asked, "You saw it, too, didn't you?"

When Isaac appeared in the doorway and came to stand beside his sister, Priscilla knew there would be no sleep until she eased the children's qualms about whatever was in the front garden. She motioned for them to lead the way toward the stairs and tried to suppress a yawn as she followed them.

The lower level was dark, and she guessed it was long past midnight. A glance toward the Muirs' house showed the brothers were asleep. The faint thought that she should wake Gilbert or one of the footmen filtered through her mind, but she did not reach for a bell. There was no sense in rousing them until she determined what had unsettled Leah and Isaac. A tent in the front garden! What nonsense.

Once they saw that they had been fooled by the moonlight, they could return to bed and sleep.

And her nice dream . . . Bother! What had it been about?

The creak of the door was so loud that she half expected it would wake the whole house, but she heard no sound of hurried footfalls. Everyone else was asleep, a very wise place to be in the middle of the night.

Two hands—one on each side—gripped her wrapper. Priscilla adjusted her children's hands so they did not tug until her collar threatened to choke her. She gave them each a comforting smile before she pushed open the door.

"Take heart," she said. "One must not be frightened of something simply because it is unknown."

Slipping out onto the steps, she heard both children gasp. She could not even make that sound as she stared at her front garden. It *was* a tent. What was this gaudy red and yellow thing doing in her garden? It was huge, almost the size of her front parlor. Such a tent should have been pitched amid the desert sands where a sheikh and his harem could rest on their journey to an oasis. How shocked Aunt Cordelia would be if she were privy to these thoughts!

"Stay here, children," Priscilla said, the very thought of her aunt giving her strength to find out why this tent was here . . . before Aunt Cordelia woke, saw it, and flew up to the boughs.

"But, Mama—" Isaac bit back the rest of his protest when she frowned at him.

"Wait here," she ordered.

"We will, but take this, Mama." Leah stepped forward and held out a walking stick she must have taken from the front hall, where a pot of them waited for anybody who wanted to use one to climb up and down the steep chalk cliffs. "Just in case."

"Thank you." She hefted the walking stick as she edged down the steps. It had a bird's head carved into the ebony, and it would serve well if she needed to defend herself.

Against whom? Who would set a *tent* up in her garden? She frowned. Mayhap that gypsy theater troupe had returned to Stonehall-on-Sea or a wagon had lagged behind and had paused for the night. She would have gladly welcomed them to use her garden, but it would have been polite for them to ask permission before raising a tent amid the boxwood.

Priscilla was halfway to the tent when she realized the wise thing to do would be to go back into the house and send one of the footmen to investigate. She paused, considered turning around, then sighed. Her own words to the children came back to haunt her. *One must not be frightened of something simply because it is unknown.* That had been so much easier to say when she was within the safe walls of Mermaid Cottage.

A flap was open on the side of the tent closest to the house. She paused in front of it and asked, "Who is within? Will you please identify yourself?"

She received no answer. Could everyone inside the tent be asleep? Hoping she was not being foolish, she peeked in.

A single lamp hanging from the peak of the tent lit only the center. Shadows gathered at the edges, but what was in the middle of the tent was enough to bring a gasp of astonishment from her. She had dismissed her thought of a Bedouin from her head. Yet the pillows spread across the floor and the scent of some sort of incense rising from a burner to her left suggested she had traveled from England to the desert wastes of Africa in a single step.

"Is anyone here?" Priscilla wished her voice had not trembled on that question.

Again no answer.

She eased into the tent, gripping the walking stick more tightly. Someone must be nearby. It would make no sense to put up a tent in her garden and then abandon it.

A man emerged from the shadows in one corner. His head was covered by a strip of fabric. He was not tall, and his complexion was dotted with freckles. He did not match any description she had ever heard of a desert sheikh. When he pressed his hands together and bowed toward the door behind her, she looked over her shoulder.

Another man stood in the doorway. He was only a silhouette, blocking out the moonlight. His shoulders were broad, and the bloused trousers tucked into his knee-high boots suggested a coiled strength.

She sucked in her breath as he took a single step toward her, his face still hidden by the shadows. Facing him, she squared her own shoulders. She concentrated on making her voice remain steady as she said, "I am Lady Priscilla Flanders, and this is my garden. I wish to know why you have raised your tent here."

The man in the doorway was silent. The one behind her made some sound that suggested he was choking. When she glanced at him, he lowered his head in another bow toward the door.

Clenching her fingers on the walking stick, she raised it enough so the man in the doorway could not fail to take note of it. "Sir, I ask you again. Why have you raised your tent here?"

"Because I didn't want to wake you in the middle of the night, Pris."

"Neville! I should have guessed."

Priscilla fought not to smile. Sir Neville Hathaway never failed to make a most outrageous entrance back into her life. She knew she should ask why he was dressed up as if about to ride off to see the pyramids, but she doubted he would give her a straightforward answer. Neville enjoyed hoaxing her. If he were not such a good friend . . . She lowered the walking stick when he glanced at it and raised a dark brow.

He laughed as he stepped into the lamplight that laced blue fire through his black hair. "By Jove, Pris, would you have beaten me senseless with that cane if I had failed to identify myself?"

"To beat one senseless suggests that the one being beaten has some sense to begin with."

He laughed, and clasping her elbow, tugged her to him. He lifted the cane from her hand. Tossing it to the man behind her, he said, "It is good to see you, Pris."

"It would be good to see you, too, Neville, if just once you would begin a call as everyone else does."

Instead of answering, he slanted his mouth across hers. The sweet sensation of his lips on hers swept away the months since she had last seen him in London. While his lips thrilled hers, her fingers slid up his loose sleeves to his shoulders. She clasped her hands behind his nape, and he showered fiery kisses across her face until she was laughing with delight.

He drew back enough to say quietly, "I trust no one else begins a call with that, Pris."

Her answer was forestalled when her right arm was plucked off Neville's shoulder.

The shorter man bowed over her fingers as he said with a strong Scottish brogue, "'Tis *my* pleasure, Lady Priscilla, to make your acquaintance."

Priscilla glanced at Neville, saw his grin, then turned to the man who was lifting off the cloth draped over his head to reveal a mass of black curls. "Good evening—" She halted herself, for the hour was long past evening.

"Duncan McAndrews," the shorter man replied as if they were meeting under the most mundane of circumstances. "Recently of Edinburgh, but now paying a call on my friend Hathaway."

"Welcome to Mermaid Cottage, Mr. McAndrews. Are you planning to stay here tonight?"

Neville answered, "I told you that we did not want to disturb you, Pris. This will be comfortable. If—"

Leah stuck her head into the tent and whistled.

Priscilla was uncertain whether to chide her younger daughter first for disobeying her or for making such an unladylike sound. She said nothing as Leah launched herself into Neville's arms, giving him a hug.

"Uncle Neville!" She laughed as he set her on her feet, then hugged him again.

He was not truly the children's uncle, for he had been her late husband's best friend for many years. Many had pondered the friendship between a parson and such a rogue, but everyone in Mermaid Cottage understood that Reverend Dr. Lazarus Flanders and Neville Hathaway—more recently Sir Neville Hathaway—paid *on dits* no mind. 'Twas a habit Priscilla wished more people would acquire.

With a giggle, Leah said, "I should have guessed it was you, Uncle Neville, when pebbles hit my window."

"Pebbles?" Priscilla asked. "I thought you did not want to bother us tonight."

"I said I had no intention of disturbing *you*. I had no idea Leah would wake you." Neville wore the smile that urged her to forgive him. She resisted it, for she wanted to know why he was here and for how long he would stay. When she asked that, he said, "Surely you have heard of the medieval Faire Lord Stenborough is hosting for Michaelmas Day. Spelled F-A-I-R-E, as I am sure you assumed."

Lord Stenborough was seldom at his dirty acres, and she could not recall the last time she had encountered him. The man, who was probably a decade older than she, had appeared at St. Elizabeth's Church when Lazarus was pastor only at Christmas and Easter. Then he had presented the church with donations for the poor as if trying to make up for ignoring it the rest of the year, although its living was his responsibility. It was said he enjoyed long hours playing cards, and his debts were many. If not for the generosity of the previous Duke of Meresden, the church would have fallen into disrepair years ago.

"Is that why a theater troupe came through Stonehall-on-Sea today . . . I mean, yesterday?" she asked as Neville held open the flap on the tent for her.

"I would guess as much. Stenborough has decided to celebrate his birthday and the quarter day in grand style. He issued invitations to half the Polite World, knowing that the other half would come along as well."

They reached the steps where Isaac still stood. Her son's noisy greeting was sure to wake up the rest of the household, a fact that was emphasized when lamplight appeared at many windows on the upper floors. Priscilla hushed him and shooed him back up the steps. His exuberance did not need to rouse the Muir brothers as well.

"Daphne's birthday is soon, too," Leah said as she skipped up the steps. "She is going to be sixteen years old."

"I know that." Neville gave Leah a smile.

"Oh, does that mean you have brought a gift for her?" She giggled. "Will you tell me what it is?"

"Possibly and no."

She gave him a fierce frown, but her pose was ruined by a wide yawn.

"Off to bed with you," Priscilla said. "You will have time enough to speak with him in the morning while he is taking down his tent."

As Leah hurried into the house, Neville asked, "Am I to believe that my tent and I are being evicted?"

"Whatever do you need with such a tent?"

He waited until she had entered the front hallway along with Mr. McAndrews before he said, "I told you about Lord Stenborough's Faire."

"You are planning to stay in that tent while you are there?" She put the walking stick back into the stone pot set on the floor. Seeing a light in the front parlor, she was not surprised when Gilbert emerged, sleep weighing on his eyelids.

After she had asked the butler to bring something to drink and any cake that remained from dessert, Neville said, "I assumed Duncan, Isaac, and I could stay in that one while you and the girls used the other one I have in the wagon out on the road. I even brought a third for your servants and—"

"Staying in tents?" she gasped. "Have you lost your mind, Neville?"

"That question comes too late," Mr. McAndrews

interjected with a laugh. "I believe he misplaced it years ago."

Neville chuckled, but his eyes rose toward the stairs.

Priscilla rolled her own eyes as her aunt came slowly down the stairs. Aunt Cordelia's cap was askew and her wrapper misbuttoned halfway down. Mentioning that would embarrass her aunt, so she hurried to introduce her to Mr. McAndrews. Her aunt and Neville needed no introduction, and Priscilla wanted to avoid daggers being drawn between them for as long as possible. She would never be able to reassure Aunt Cordelia that Neville was not a horrid influence on the children, and she would never persuade Neville that her aunt truly meant well with all her intrusions and comments.

As Aunt Cordelia glowered in their direction, Neville said, "To answer your question, Pris, the tent is because the distance to Stenborough's estate is too long for you and the children to be traveling back and forth each day. As the invitation did not include an offer to enjoy living beneath his roof—and I believe he anticipates too many in attendance even for his house—I thought I would provide a proper roof for us."

"Proper?"

"Mayhap I should have said appropriate."

"You are assuming we will be attending."

"How can you resist such an invitation?" he asked, smiling.

"I received none from Lord Stenborough."

"I meant mine, Pris."

She wanted to retort, but that tempting smile was working its sorcery on her again. Neville was the most exasperating man she knew. Yet her life was flavorless without him in it, mixing her and the children up in his peculiar ways of tweaking society's nose.

Taking her hands, he folded them between his. "Do come to the Faire, Pris. What better way to prepare to celebrate Daphne's upcoming birthday than for all of us to have some time together?" His grin became rakish as he added in a near whisper, "And for the two of us to have some time together."

"You said Mr. McAndrews would be going with you as well."

"Yes, I brought him along for your aunt."

"For Aunt Cordelia?"

"I have told you multiple times, Pris, that your aunt needs something other than your son to keep her busy. I figured, why not Duncan McAndrews? He is a good chap and has stood up to viragoes before. In fact, he rather fancies them."

She glanced at where the short, dark-haired man was bowing over her aunt's hand. Aunt Cordelia was wearing a smile that hinted she had already acceded to the idea of having Mr. McAndrews pay court to her.

"A brilliant idea, if I say so myself," Neville murmured. "Now you and the children can enjoy the Faire with me. What do you say, Pris?"

TWO

What else could she have said but yes?

Priscilla thought about that as she rode in Neville's fine open carriage toward Stenborough Park. The house was set back so far from the road that any passersby would not have guessed it existed. Unlike the houses built in the past century as a showcase for their owners' wealth and good taste, this estate had once been a fortified castle. The crenellations still edged the top of the walls, and a dry moat was crossed by a bridge that had replaced the gate. Now the moat was filled with flowering shrubs, and a long avenue of ancient trees welcomed guests.

Since being built in the twelfth century, the house had been added on to and redone so many times that the crenellations and the moat were the only outward signs of its age. The windows that were edged with ivy were wide and tall rather than the arrow slits of the past. Doors were thrown open to receive the breeze off the sea and the viscount's guests.

"There is the Faire," Daphne said, turning to look forward.

"Do not gawk," chided Aunt Cordelia. "It is not becoming."

Daphne sat back as if her aunt had shoved her.

Folding her hands on her lap, she said, "Forgive me, Aunt Cordelia."

When her aunt flashed a superior smile, Priscilla fought not to laugh. Her aunt had never had children. Otherwise, she would see how transparent Daphne's motives were. Her older daughter was willing to accept any scold in the hope that her great-aunt would become her ally in compelling Priscilla to fire Daphne off in the next Season.

Priscilla did not intend to think of that now. She wanted to enjoy the anticipation of the Faire. The day was sunny and surprisingly warm for this time of year. Neville was riding his horse while they used his carriage. This outing would give her a chance to see friends from town and for the children to learn a bit of history. On the latter, she was sure there would not be much to learn. Hiring actors to portray people from the Middle Ages suggested accuracy was not what Lord Stenborough sought.

The entertainments would be many, Neville had told her while the younger children squealed with delight. Animals, fortune-tellers and magicians, and even a masquerade ball the final night of the celebrations. When Priscilla had suggested they would not attend the masquerade because there was no time to prepare, he told her that he had already arranged to have costumes for them. They would be delivered on the morrow. She had no doubts about the fit. Neville never failed to notice everything about everyone around him.

"Do you think there will be a dungeon at the Faire like the one in the cellars of Stenborough Park?" asked Isaac, starting to rise before a glance from his aunt warned him to remain still.

"You should not heed rumors," Priscilla said with a laugh.

"Rumors? Everyone in Stonehall-on-Sea knows that Lord Stenborough's family still has the torture equipment they used to use."

"Sometimes the things everyone knows are still nonsense." She hurried to add when he looked crestfallen, "However, who knows what the Faire might have?"

His grin returning, Isaac scampered out of the carriage before it had completely halted in front of the red and yellow tent. It was set at the edge of an open field facing the grand house. Calling a reprimand after her son would not curb his exuberance, so Priscilla did not bother. He poked his head into the tent and was racing to the blue and red one next to it before anyone else stepped down from the carriage.

"May I?" Neville asked, appearing on the other side.

Priscilla stared at him as she had at the tent last night. She had not expected to see Neville dressed in a costume that he might have worn in some production of Shakespeare's works. Beneath his red-lined cloak, his black waistcoat appeared to be of velvet, and its slashed sleeves were edged with gold. A full-sleeved white shirt, probably the one he had been wearing last night, was under it. A small ruff was beneath his chin. His breeches of the same gold as the stitching on his sleeves were sedate in style, and his knee-high boots shone brightly.

Bowing his head, he put on a narrow-brimmed hat decorated with a blue feather. He held up his hand to Aunt Cordelia with as much aplomb as if he always dressed this way.

"Thank you," her aunt said. It was reluctant gratitude, but a good sign that the day might go well. That Aunt Cordelia was willing to let Neville assist her out of the carriage suggested she was in a festive mood.

Priscilla motioned for her daughters to wait while Aunt Cordelia stepped down. Her aunt moved away from Neville with haste. That neither Neville nor her aunt spoke other than pleasantries further buoyed her expectations of a good day. Even Neville's surreptitious wink as he handed her down before turning to help Daphne and Leah added to her anticipation. Mayhap Neville had been correct in bringing Mr. McAndrews—or Duncan as the short man insisted they all call him.

"Everything is set," Neville said. With a broad gesture, he motioned toward the red and yellow tent. "Your costumes are waiting in there, ladies."

"Costumes?" Daphne's eyes glowed with excitement. "We are wearing costumes, too?"

"Your gowns may be *de rigueur* for this century, but are not appropriate for the sixteenth century. Go ahead."

Priscilla smiled as they hurried toward the tent. "You have made this a grand outing for the children, Neville."

"And you?" He drew her hand within his arm. As they walked between the carriage and the wagon carrying the maid and footman and their bags, he chuckled. "I thought *you* would enjoy this, too."

"I believe I shall, now that you and my aunt seem to be in good pax."

"A situation I fear is temporary."

"Neville." She paused and faced him. "Please refrain from driving her into a pelter."

"Me?" He pressed his hand to his black doublet as he gave her a disingenuous smile that did not fit on his strictly sculptured face. "You wound me, Pris, with your assumption that *I* shall begin the next brangle."

"I am simply assuming you will be the cause of it."

He chuckled. "Most likely, for she finds fault in even a 'Good morning' from me."

"Then simply nod to her."

"I shall endeavor to be the pattern-card of kindness to your aunt." He glanced at the tent. "Why don't you change? Then we can search for Duncan. Once we find him, we shall let Stenborough know we have arrived."

When Priscilla went into the tent, closing the flap behind her, Neville stepped aside to stay out of the way of her servants. He chuckled. June was smiling at Juster, the footman. He wondered if Priscilla was aware of the growing attraction between the two.

In less time than he had expected it would take, the flap was pushed aside again. He watched when Daphne, then Leah emerged. Their pastel gowns were cut in a simple style, the skirts split to reveal the underdress. Daphne in rose and Leah in yellow were busy admiring each other's gowns. He paid them no more attention as the flap opened again, and Priscilla emerged.

Her gown was a deep red fustian with a diamond pattern of gold stitched across the bodice. Like his sleeves, hers were slashed, but pink and white brocade peeked through as it did on her slashed skirt. The deep square neckline showed off a gold locket with a single pearl in the center. A high collar arched up behind her head to frame her face in stiff, white lace.

"Bother!" she said, reaching up and unhooking the collar from the shoulders of her gown. "Having this on gives me sympathy for horses wearing blinders."

"A proper Elizabethan lady would wear it," he replied.

"Then I fear I shall be a most improper one." She handed the collar to her maid, who stared at it, clearly trying to guess what she should do with it.

"I thought that might be the case." He gave a quick order to June, who disappeared into the smallest of the quartet of tents.

"Otherwise the dress is lovely, Neville," Priscilla said. "Thank you for getting these for us."

"Do take good care of them. I promised Morton that I would return the costumes to the theater in the same condition as when I borrowed them."

"Your friend Morton seems to have an endless collection of costumes."

Instead of answering, he turned when June came forward with a box. He had put it into the wagon with the rest of the bags, suspecting Priscilla would find the collar unmanageable. With a smile, he plucked a hairpin from Priscilla's sedate chignon.

"What are you doing?" she gasped, reaching for the pin.

"If you are not going to be a proper Elizabethan lady, then I believe you should have the look of an improper one." He withdrew a second pin, and gold curls fell down her back. "Don't say it, Pris."

"I must. What will be thought if I wear my hair down on my shoulders? I am not a child."

"That is quite true, and I know your next argument will be that a parson's widow and the mother of three children should not wear her hair loose." He drew out the last pin, and the rest of her hair cas-

caded around her, dropping nearly to her waist. He
tossed the pins into the box and lifted out a garland
of dried flowers. Gently he placed it on her head.
"There. Now you look perfect for the Faire."

As her daughters giggled while she adjusted the
circlet of daisies and pink roses on her hair, he enjoyed admiring her. He would have liked to draw her
nearer so he could sift his fingers through her hair,
but too many people were nearby.

Daphne and Leah excused themselves when they
saw some young girls emerging from a closed carriage. They went to greet their friends with Aunt
Cordelia, still wearing her customary gown, following after them. More giggles rushed back as the girls
greeted each other.

Saying nothing, but glad that Lady Cordelia had
found something other than Priscilla to keep her
busy, Neville settled Priscilla's hand on his arm. She
gathered up her skirt and walked with him in the opposite direction.

He edged around the collection of tents. The
troupe's wagons were on the far side of the field. Between, on the already trampled grass would be the
Faire. Buildings and tents were being raised, and he
heard wisps of music someone was practicing. Something that was, he assumed, supposed to be a castle
had high walls reaching out in an arc on either side
of it. Seeing more carriages along the avenue, he
guessed the number of people here to celebrate
Stenborough's birthday and Michaelmas Day would
be even more than he had heard whispered. The
whole of the *ton* might not be in attendance, but it
would seem so when everyone crowded onto the
field.

"This is amazing," Priscilla said. "I had no idea,

even after seeing the wagons, the celebration would be this grand."

"Stenborough never does anything halfheartedly. When he married, you would have guessed one of the royal family was about to take a wife. A golden carriage and six white horses." He chuckled. "The man wagers the same way. If he had not inherited such a fortune, he would have run through it years ago."

"Which way should we look for Duncan?" She drew in a deep breath. "Whatever is cooking smells delicious."

"Our midday meal, I suspect. Let's go toward the wagons. Duncan is most likely in that direction, sticking his nose into whatever catches his attention. A reason I believe he and your aunt will get along well."

"Neville, recall yourself!" she chided as they stepped into the maze of small tents and hastily erected buildings and stages.

"I am recalling *them*. They are much alike. Duncan always wishes to know what is planned. He is not a man who likes surprises."

Neville slowed at a loud curse. It was not only loud, but angry. When another man answered, his words as heated, Neville led Priscilla away. He had no interest in the troupe's bickerings.

A brown-haired man carrying a sheaf of papers appeared around the edge of a tent and almost collided with them. He hastily stepped back and began to apologize. The quality of his voice and his costume revealed he probably was not part of this theater company.

That was confirmed when the slender man said,

"Excuse me. I am Garvin Harmsworth, Lord Stenborough's estate manager."

"Lady Priscilla Flanders," Neville said, with a nod toward her.

"My lady." Harmsworth bowed over her hand and bobbed back up like a leaf floating on water. "And I know you are Sir Neville Hathaway."

"You do?" He had not suspected his reputation had preceded him to Stenborough Park.

"Mr. McAndrews mentioned that I should be watching for you because you would be interested in a tour of the Faire's grounds. He mentioned you would be particularly interested in the tournament grounds and the dunking pond."

"So he could do what when you were not watching?"

Harmsworth's narrow face barely held his wide eyes. "Are you suggesting Mr. McAndrews is seeking to create some mischief? Oh, dear, that will not please Lord Stenborough. Lord Stenborough wishes his guests to have a good time at the Faire, you realize, but—"

"He does not wish the mischief to begin until he can join in?" asked Neville.

Harmsworth sputtered like a bird fluffing out its feathers and was calmed only when Priscilla said, "I believe Neville is jesting, Mr. Harmsworth."

"Oh." He placed the pages under his arm as if they were a riding crop. "Very amusing, Sir Neville."

"Yes, very." Neville smiled. "Could you tell us where we might find Lord Stenborough?"

"Lord Stenborough will be welcoming his guests at the midday feast."

"Over there?" asked Priscilla, looking to her left. Neville followed her glance toward an area that was roped off. Canvas large enough to serve as the mainsail of a ship was stretched over tables. Even through the shadows, he could see people working among them.

"Yes," Harmsworth said. "The preparations are nearly complete. Would you like something cool to drink before you continue your walk around the Faire?"

"How pleasant," Priscilla answered before Neville could. "A cool drink, I hope."

He glanced at her outfit, then smiled. "It is such a warm day, isn't it? Come this way."

As they followed, Priscilla noticed Neville's eyes were twinkling with anticipation. Mr. Harmsworth had been worried about Duncan causing mischief. Rather, he should have considered what Neville might do. She smiled. Whatever it was was sure to be interesting. Her life would no longer be quiet now that Neville had come back into it.

A crowd was gathering among the faux buildings that appeared as if they would collapse in a gust off the sea. Walking past members of the theater troupe, Priscilla saw Neville looking closely at them.

"Anyone you know?" she asked quietly.

"Possibly."

"Yon lass appears to be eager to make your acquaintance." She laughed when his head swiveled to see the woman watching them intently. The woman wore colorful robes and what appeared to be coins hanging off a scarf tied around her head. She went into a tiny tent and drew the flap down over its doorway. "Or mayhap not."

"Amusing, Pris."

"Yes, very," she replied as he had to Mr. Harmsworth.

He grimaced, then smiled. "By Jove, Pris, it is good to see you."

"It is, isn't it?"

Neville was given no opportunity to answer as Mr. Harmsworth began a listing of the guests attending. Priscilla was uncertain if Lord Stenborough's estate manager was hoping to impress them or simply impress all the names on his own mind.

Instead of going toward the wagons decorated with brightly colored flags hanging sullenly in the morning sunshine, Mr. Harmsworth led them to a gray plank wall several feet taller than Neville. It was part of the castle. The sound of hammers came from the other side.

When he paused, Priscilla was astonished to see him open a door in the wall. It had been so well camouflaged she could have walked past without noticing it.

"Lady Priscilla?" Mr. Harmsworth bowed slightly as he held the gate open. He straightened and exclaimed, "Mr. McAndrews!"

Duncan wore a broad smile that seemed to fit him better than his fur-lined cloak and tunic. Priscilla wondered what century he was supposed to represent, then reminded herself that her own costume was far from authentic.

"Isn't it a lovely day?" gushed Duncan. "The perfect day for revelry."

"You believe every day is the perfect day for revelry," Neville said.

"True, so true." He smiled at Priscilla. "May I assume your charming aunt is also here?"

"Yes. We all arrived together."

"How splendid! Isn't it splendid, Neville?"

"Very."

Priscilla tried not to laugh. Neville had been sincere when he said he thought she would enjoy the Faire. She took a step forward to follow Mr. Harmsworth, then halted when the stiff front of her gown cut into her.

"Sorry," said Duncan with a sheepish expression as she looked over her shoulder. "I fear I stepped on your train, Lady Priscilla."

"I am afraid we all will be tripping over one another because we are not accustomed to such trains except in court dress. Let me get this out of the way." Bending, she scooped up some of the thick material. "After all—"

Something whizzed over Priscilla's head. Neville yanked her down. She heard shouts as she struck the hard earth.

"Neville, have you taken a knock in the cradle?" She tried to push away from him.

"Don't move," he ordered.

"Don't move? What are you prattling about?"

"That." He pointed to where a knife had struck the door at the height of her heart.

THREE

Priscilla stared at the knife, which was still quivering in the wood. She heard Duncan's gasp and Mr. Harmsworth's curse, but she could only stare. If she had not bent to gather up her dress . . .

Neville brought her to her feet. "How are you?"

"I am fine. If *this* is your idea of finding ways for me to enjoy this Faire—"

"Don't be absurd, Pris." His slitted eyes scanned the field. "I would never be so frivolous as to put you in such danger."

She nodded. If Neville had arranged for someone to scare a year from her life, he would be laughing now. Instead, he was furious.

"Lady Priscilla, do you wish to sit?" asked Mr. Harmsworth. His hand settled on her arm, but she stepped away to look at the knife.

A brawny hand at the end of a hairy arm stretched in front of her, plucking the blade from the wood. She faced a man whose short-sleeved costume emphasized his muscles. There was nothing attractive about this hulk of a man whose nose had been on the end of too many losing fights.

"May I assume that knife is yours?" she asked.

Neville stepped between her and the huge man. "Are you mad? You could have killed Lady Priscilla."

The man eyed both of them, then shrugged. "If I 'ad been aimin' at 'er, I'd 'ave 'it 'er. I weren't aimin' at 'er." He gave Mr. Harmsworth a snide smile.

The slighter man gulped, but he jutted his chin. A want-witted motion, Priscilla thought, for it was an invitation for the big man to slam his fist into it. Mr. Harmsworth would be about as effectual in fisticuffs against him as a terrier barking at the heels of a horse.

Even so, Mr. Harmsworth's voice was sharp. "Birch, I warned you yesterday about being careful where you practice."

"Like I told the gent, I wouldn't 'ave 'it 'er." Birch's voice was surprisingly high-pitched coming from such a barrel chest. "I can skin the fuzz off a fly's wing from fifty feet."

"Now, there is a useful skill," murmured Neville.

Mr. Harmsworth snapped, "I do not care if you can give it a shave. You must not throw that knife around the viscount's guests, or you will have to leave. You have been warned once already."

Birch grumbled a curse and shoved Mr. Harmsworth aside. Duncan moved back before his foot was stepped on.

Mr. Harmsworth brushed off his velvet sleeve. "Why don't you return to work so you can pretend this troupe is worth what it is being paid?"

Birch stamped away.

"I am sorry you had to witness that," Mr. Harmsworth said. "These people are used to a rougher life. You know how actors are."

"Yes, I do," Neville said.

Priscilla thought he might be trying to lighten the situation, but he was enraged. At Birch for his foolish disregard for those around him or at Mr. Harmsworth for his derogatory comments about thespians? Although Neville had not been on stage in many years, he maintained friendships in the London theaters.

"It will not happen again," Mr. Harmsworth said, showing he was unaware of Neville's reaction. "If you will come this way . . ." He motioned toward a stone wall leading into a garden.

"How do you fare, Pris?" asked Neville as Duncan walked with Mr. Harmsworth.

Priscilla watched Birch weave an uneven path across the open field. The man reeked of cheap beer and too many days without a bath, but she could not mistake his intentions. The knife had been to get Mr. Harmsworth's attention.

"Pris?"

"You already asked me how I was doing," she answered, looking back at Neville.

"And you answered when Duncan and Harmsworth could hear. Now tell me the truth."

"I feel like that fly that has been skinned," she said with a weak smile. "If all the actors in this troupe are so careless, this could be a very dangerous place."

"I will speak to Bennett."

"Who?"

"He is the manager of this troupe."

"I thought you were unsure if you knew anyone among them."

He smiled and drew her arm through his. "I was speaking of the actors. I knew Bennett when he was working in London. He is a decent fellow, and he will not want anyone to be injured because he knows at whose feet the blame will be laid."

Her frown fell away as she put her other hand on his arm. "I suppose I would have been surprised if you had not known at least one person here."

Mr. Harmsworth motioned for them to hurry.

With the grass trying to trip her on every step, Priscilla walked with Neville to where the estate manager and Duncan were starting down some stone steps. She was astonished to see one wing of the house not far from them. Stenborough Park must be even larger than she had guessed.

A stone gazebo was set in the middle of a garden that had few flowers remaining. Benches followed the columns parading around in a circle. Stepping in, she gasped when her dress cut her across the stomach again. She turned. The hem was wedged between the stone edge of a bench. She jerked on it, but the fabric was even more obstinate than she was.

"Allow me."

Neville knelt and freed the material. "I have never been able to resist playing Sir Walter Raleigh. Mud puddles and lovely ladies are my life." He chuckled as he stood.

Mr. Harmsworth went to a table in the middle of the gazebo and picked up a sweating pitcher. He poured glasses of lemonade and held them out.

Instead of taking one, Duncan said, "I would prefer to explore more. If you will excuse me, I shall rejoin you at the midday feast." He bowed his head. "Good morning, Lady Priscilla."

"Duncan can never sit still long," Neville said as his friend hurried back through the garden at a speed that implied a hangman was on his heels. "He is as eager to look around as Isaac."

Mr. Harmsworth's name was bellowed.

He flinched. "Lord Stenborough is seeking me. I must ask you to excuse me, as well."

Priscilla wondered if the estate manager would flee or go to meet his employer, but Mr. Harmsworth had no chance to do either before a man stormed into the gazebo.

He had squeezed himself into a fur-trimmed, red doublet that he wore with dark blue stockings. It was not a flattering ensemble for a man who had not escaped his childhood pudginess. He opened his mouth to say something, then seemed to take note of her standing there.

"Lord Stenborough," he said, taking her hand and bowing over it. His motion revealed a bald spot covered by a few sparse, dark hairs. "And who are you, my dear?"

"This is Lady Priscilla Flanders," Mr. Harmsworth answered quickly. "Her companion is Sir Neville Hathaway."

"Hathaway?" The viscount's smile broadened. "I had hoped you would accept the invitation." His gaze boldly swept over Priscilla. "And you brought a lovely friend with you."

"Actually, I brought many friends." Neville wondered how he could have forgotten what a doddering rake Stenborough was. Mayhap because he never had been the one escorting a lady who caught the viscount's appreciative eye. He had heard complaints about Stenborough's assumption that every woman would welcome his attentions.

"Yes," Priscilla said, her smile warm, although her fingers were digging into his arm, warning him that she found Stenborough vexing. "My children are very eager to join in with the celebrations, Lord Stenborough."

"Children?" The viscount recalled himself, and his smile became tight. "I am so glad you brought them. I trust I will see them during the next few days."

Neville swallowed his laugh, but it almost escaped

when he saw Harmsworth's mouth working. The estate manager was enjoying the sight of his employer struggling to regain his composure. Even though he had suspected before that Harmsworth's loyalty was based more on his own comfort than Stenborough's, Neville was certain of it now.

After draining his glass, he set it on the table beside the pitcher. He saw Priscilla take a sip before she put hers next to his. When she glanced at him, she nodded although he had said nothing. Trust Pris to know what he was thinking. She could most of the time, but fortunately not all the time. No woman should be privy to a man's every thought, especially the ones he had about her that he was not yet ready to reveal.

"We will leave you to your discussion with Mr. Harmsworth," Priscilla said with a smile that could melt the hardest hearts. After all, it had his own.

"I did not intend to chase you away." Stenborough was again composed, although his eyes continued to appraise her to discern if she was interested in an *affaire de coeur* with him.

"Of course you didn't. I know how busy you must be. I assume this is a very important birthday for you, Lord Stenborough."

"Yes." His voice became crisp, and Neville again had to fight not to laugh. That single word revealed so much. Stenborough was not pleased time was passing, carrying him further from his youth.

Neville said exactly that as he strolled with Priscilla to where the Faire's preparations had taken on a frantic urgency as more guests wandered among the tents and buildings.

"Show our host some sympathy, Neville," Priscilla replied.

"Sympathy? I daresay he envisions himself very

much the roué whose title and lard-filled pockets will turn a young girl's head."

"I am not a young girl, so you need not fret on my behalf."

"You? Pris, I am very aware how readily you can take care of yourself."

"Then do not puff up like a frog when Lord Stenborough cocks an eye at me."

"I did not."

"I shan't argue that, although if I had had a looking glass, I would have gladly shown you." She glanced to her right. "I am pleased to see no sign of Mr. Birch. He might have been honest with his boasts, but that knife was too close."

"He would be want-witted to throw it so close to a guest again."

"I doubt anyone has ever described him as wise."

"More likely boorish."

When she smiled—at last—Neville did as well. He allowed her to change the subject to the odd buildings. He was more interested in the people. Not just those who would be portraying the medieval characters for the guests' entertainment; he was intrigued with the guests themselves.

Wandering amid the garish tents, he had to own the performers were skilled. Jugglers tossed balls and sticks and a hat they plucked off an unsuspecting man's head. Jesters pranced with their beribboned scepters that were topped with miniature heads or an animal. Music came from the building that was supposed to be a castle. It was dwarfed by Stenborough Park's sprawling wings. The bell in its highest tower began to chime. He counted to twelve, then looked at the sky.

"It must be time for the midday feast," Priscilla

said as the crowd moved toward the fake castle like sheep being herded by invisible dogs.

"Then we should not delay. Duncan will be looking for us. He will not forgive me for being late, especially when there is food waiting."

"It is going to take some time to get that crowd through the small gate."

"Then we should go around the back way," he said.

"Where is the back way?"

He shrugged.

"Then how do you know there is a back way?"

"There always is. All we need to do is find it. It should take far less time than trying to get through that mob."

She smiled. "Before we go that back way, we need to find the children and Aunt Cordelia."

That took less time than Neville had guessed, because there were not many children among the guests. He smiled as Isaac chattered about all he had seen, and he had apparently seen most of the Faire already, poking his nose and fingers into whatever caught his fancy. The girls were jubilant. Even Lady Cordelia was smiling, although she still wore a gown suited for the present rather than the past and carried a parasol. Priscilla had assured him that her aunt had a warm heart, but Lady Cordelia seldom revealed it when he was near.

Priscilla was not surprised when Neville led them through the door Mr. Harmsworth had opened. Mr. Harmsworth and a young woman stood on the far side. The black-haired woman's wide skirt was a collection of outrageous colors. Below an ebony veil decorated with coins, her thin face was lengthened with a scowl.

Neville chuckled. "Orysia, I see you are still playing a gypsy."

She whirled, and the skirt belled more around her. Her eyes, lined with kohl, grew round. "Neville Hathaway, you are the very man I need!"

"She speaks her mind, doesn't she?" Priscilla laughed softly. "Or is she jesting?"

Under his breath, Neville warned, "As I recall, Orysia does not have a sense of humor."

"A friend of yours?" asked Aunt Cordelia with an outraged sniff. "I should have guessed as much. Come along." She started to stamp away, then paused when no one else moved.

Priscilla said, "Go with Aunt Cordelia, children."

Daphne started, "But, Mama—"

"Take your brother and sister and look for Mr. McAndrews, so we can dine together. Then we shall explore the Faire together." She put her hand on her eldest's arm and smiled. "Doesn't that sound like fun?"

"More fun than having Aunt Cordelia annoyed with us."

Kissing her daughter on the cheek, Priscilla watched as Daphne led Leah and Isaac to where their great-aunt was waiting with little patience. Then Priscilla looked at the woman dressed like a gypsy who was regarding Neville just as impatiently.

Neville said, "Pris, this is Orysia Aleksandovicheva. Orysia, Lady Priscilla Flanders."

The woman did not look at her. "Neville—"

"You should address him as 'Sir Neville,'" Mr. Harmsworth said sharply.

"*Sir* Neville, is it?" Orysia smiled. "My, haven't some of us done well for ourselves?"

"It requires only having the right relatives," Neville replied.

She laughed, then pointed to Mr. Harmsworth. "Mayhap, *Sir* Neville, you can talk some sense into him. He will not heed me."

"What is wrong?"

"What is wrong?" Orysia repeated, her voice rising on each word. "Let me tell you what is wrong! He has insisted that I put my tent at the far end of the Faire. How will I have any customers?"

"Customers?" asked Priscilla.

Orysia—Priscilla must think of her that way because she doubted if she could repeat the woman's surname—frowned at her.

"She fancies herself a great seer into the future," Mr. Harmsworth said.

"Fancies?" Orysia rounded on him. "If you doubt me, you need only to listen to what I tell you of *your* future. If you are brave enough to heed what I have to say." Folding her arms in front of her, she said, "Lord Stenborough promised me that I would have my tent near the center of the Faire's grounds. He has been very kind to me."

"I will discuss that with him after the feast."

"Don't you believe me?" She looked at Neville. "Do tell him I would not lie."

Neville nodded. "I have never heard Orysia tell a lie when she knows she might be caught."

Priscilla could not restrain her laugh. "Forgive me," she said.

"Why are you asking to be forgiven when you have done nothing wrong?" Orysia smiled. "Come to my tent later, my lady, and I will see what my cards show for you."

"I know what the future holds," Neville said.

"Trouble if we are any later meeting Duncan and your aunt."

Orysia's smile warmed. "You should come to my tent, *Sir* Neville. I shall read for you, too."

He nodded, but said when they were out of earshot, "Stay away from her, Pris."

"Advice you are going to take for yourself?"

"Is that jealousy I hear in your voice?"

"I believe you have let the fantasy of this Faire unsettle your mind."

Slipping his arm around her waist, he said, "Fantasies? Yes, but not about this Faire."

She ran her fingertips along his cheek. She would have preferred to touch him further, but she could not forget the people crowded into this Faire. To do anything untoward would reflect poorly on her children and earn her a public reprimand from her aunt. Yet she could not halt her fingers from brushing his lips.

He kissed them gently before putting his finger beneath her chin and tipping her face toward his. "Shall we do a bit of exploring of our own later?"

"Far from Orysia's tent, I assume."

"Far from her tent and your aunt and the children and our host and . . ." He smiled. "Shall we?"

"Yes, I believe we shall." She did not want to step back, but she did. "They are waiting for us now."

"Pris, one of these days, I am going to budge you from that horrible habit of doing as you should all the time."

She laughed. "Just refrain from doing so when Isaac is near. I have been trying to impress on him that he *should* do the right thing all the time."

"I am not suggesting the wrong thing. I am suggesting a very right thing."

Her breath caught as she gazed into his ebony eyes. She did not need a suggestion, for her thoughts had wandered too often in this direction since her last visit to London and the time she had spent with him. When he offered his arm, she put her hand on it. She said nothing and he was silent as well while they walked toward the huge yellow tent.

"This way," he said.

"Are you sure?"

"Any way is better than through that crowd."

She started to agree, then heard music being played by excellent musicians. Luscious aromas assaulted her, making her realize how hungry she was. As Neville lifted a flap and motioned for her to enter, she almost bumped into a rotund man who was adjusting his costume while swearing with rare skill. She untwisted the belt he was trying to tie around him to hold a gold brocade coat over his purple doublet.

He turned, and his brown eyes widened. The apple cheeks above his black beard puffed out in a smile as he asked in a deep voice, "And who are you, lady fair?"

"Lady Priscilla Flanders," Neville answered before Priscilla could.

"Thank you, Lady Priscilla." He gave a hearty laugh. "I am honored to have a lady help me."

"Are you the king for the banquet?"

"Yes."

"Let me guess." She tapped her cheek as if in deep thought. "You must be King Henry the Eighth."

A belly laugh erupted from him. Rubbing his hand over his brush of whiskers, he said, "To tell you the truth, Lady Priscilla, I am more accurately Roland the First. However, today I play the part of that oft-wed monarch."

"Roland?" Neville grasped the man's arm. "Roland Judson?"

He squinted at Neville, and Priscilla guessed he should be wearing spectacles. "Hathaway? What are *you* doing here? I thought you had retired from the theater."

"I am here as a guest."

"Ah, that is right. You are a fine milord now, aren't you?" He gestured toward the other side of the tent. "There are plenty of roles to play if you so wish."

"I am happy to be in the audience for this performance. I shall leave the marrying and beheading to you."

"Do you have your six wives here?" asked Priscilla. "You could have two beheadings. Anne Boleyn in the morning and Catherine Howard in the afternoon."

Neville shuddered with exaggerated disgust. "Have you always had this gruesome flair, Pris?"

"I am afraid I am learning it from Isaac."

"Don't make the comment it front of the boy, or he will volunteer to be the swordsman slicing off heads."

With a laugh, Roland slapped his hand against the tent pole so hard Priscilla half-expected the canvas to fall on them. A trumpet sounded.

"You will have to excuse me," he said, abruptly serious. Adjusting his costume over his broad belly, he added, "The play begins."

Priscilla watched as he pushed past the flap to the blaring fanfare of a single trumpeter. When Neville held it open for her to follow, she slipped through and edged toward a dozen long tables crowded with guests.

"Do you see them?" she asked, amazed because she had not realized so many people were attending the Faire.

"Not yet."

"Look for Aunt Cordelia's parasol. She will—"

A scream ripped through Priscilla's bones. Then another and another and another. A deeper voice shouted for help.

Neville ran to the tables. She ran after him, each hysterical scream making her legs churn more rapidly. Who was screaming and why? Where were her children? The shrieks were not theirs, but were they all right?

He leaped over the rope separating the tables from the stage. She started to do the same; then, with an epithet as earthy in her time as in the Middle Ages, she bent to slip beneath it. She shook off a hand on her arm. She was not going to be stopped. She had to get to her children.

The screams did not stop. A woman! Pushing through the crowd, Priscilla did not apologize when she stepped on a foot. Everybody seemed frozen, save for the woman whose screeching rang through her head.

Then Priscilla burst out of the crowd. A scream within her slammed against her chest. Facedown, with a long arrow protruding from his back, was Duncan McAndrews. His head was turned toward her, his lips tilted in astonishment. His eyes were closed and his arms flung forward with the force of the arrow.

She heard more shrieks and turned to see Roland toppling to the ground, an arrow stuck in his chest.

"Run!" someone shouted. "Run before we all are killed."

FOUR

"Mama!"

Priscilla recognized her younger daughter's voice. Leah sounded terrified. Where was she? And Isaac and Daphne and Aunt Cordelia?

She tried to keep her footing as the guests fled, shoving into each other in their desperation to escape the bowman. Who had the bow?

She pushed aside her curiosity. She had to get help for Duncan. She ran to his side. When arms wrapped around her waist, she flinched, then looked down to see her son. His sisters and her very wan aunt stood behind him.

"Aunt Cordelia?" she whispered.

Somehow, her aunt heard or mayhap she simply understood, because she took the younger children by the hands. She motioned to Daphne to follow.

"Go," Priscilla said. "Watch over them."

"You think . . . ?" Daphne gulped.

Hugging Daphne, she urged, "Just go."

Priscilla bent toward Duncan. Out of the corner of her eye, she saw Neville kneeling by Roland.

"Somebody get a doctor!" When nobody moved, she pointed to a young man in a purple page's costume. "You! Find Lord Stenborough, and have him send for a doctor. Immediately!"

The boy nodded and pushed through the crowd.

Priscilla reached to check Duncan's pulse. She had not seen so much blood since—she could not think of that now. A hand settled on her arm. She tried to brush it away, but fingers tightened on her. She looked back at Neville's strained face. She flinched. He had been there the last time she had seen this much blood.

"How is Roland?" she asked.

"Dead." He tugged on her arm. "Pris, come away from Duncan."

"Let me check him. He might be—"

"No."

"Neville, I—"

His brows lowered. "Pris, you cannot help him. He is dead."

"No, he is not dead," Priscilla argued.

As if Duncan had been listening, he took a shuddering breath and moaned.

She grasped Neville's sleeve. "I sent a boy to find Lord Stenborough and have a doctor brought. Will you get a doctor before Duncan *is* dead?"

"What is going on here?" asked Lord Stenborough as he shoved through the crowd.

"Thank heavens! Get a doctor *now!*" she pleaded.

"A doctor? Now see here, Lady Priscilla. You do not give orders—"

"Get a doctor before this man dies!" She motioned toward Duncan, who was groaning.

Lord Stenborough stared, his mouth dropping. "Who is that?"

"A friend of mine," Neville said. "Will you send for a doctor?"

Lord Stenborough fired off a dozen orders that added to the confusion.

Priscilla grabbed his arm. "Get a doctor! Now!"

Neville stripped her fingers from Lord Stenborough's sleeve. While he seconded her order, she pulled a cloth from a table. She held it over Duncan as if it were a parasol. It protected him from curious eyes. She did move until an unfamiliar voice asked her to step aside. She drew the cloth away, and swallowed roughly when she heard someone gasp in horror.

It was the man behind her. He was taller than Neville but had hair the same color as hers. He wore a dark coat and carried a bag of the same stygian shade.

"Dr. Dommel is another guest," murmured Neville as he drew her aside. "Let him do what he can, Pris."

She dropped the cloth on a bench. When Neville stepped between her and where the doctor was working, she knew he would not move aside even if she asked. She wanted to lean her forehead against his shoulder and shut out everything.

"The children?" he asked.

"With my aunt. She will watch over them."

"How are you?"

"Do not fret about me. I am all right."

"Just don't swoon and get in the doctor's way."

"I do not swoon."

"I know." He kept his arm around her shoulders as she heard Dr. Dommel give orders to have Duncan taken to the house.

The doctor added, "Please leave, Sir Neville, so I can tend to this man."

"If we can—"

"Go! Removing this arrow does not require an audience."

Now Priscilla pulled on Neville's arm. They must allow the doctor to do what he could. When she saw

Neville's anguish, she wished she knew the words to offer him comfort. She was startled when an unmistakable woman rushed into the tent.

Orysia pressed her long fingers to her ruby-painted lips. "I heard screams. I had no idea—"

"You should have, if you are a psychic," Neville retorted.

"Neville," Priscilla whispered, "don't focus your frustration and fury on her."

He nodded.

Priscilla was astonished. Since she had first met him, he had always had a comment to make, even under the most horrible situations. But none of them had been as horrible as seeing his friend with an arrow in his back.

Neville shouldered aside the tent flap. It was stiflingly hot within and silent. If any of the guests had left, he had not seen sign of it. The area was crowded, even though no one was doing anything but waiting. He was unsure for what. Mayhap it was as simple as that they did not want to depart until they knew whether or not Duncan McAndrews would live.

He slapped the flat of his hand against the tent pole. *He* had invited Duncan to this debacle. Not because he thought his friend would enjoy it, but to keep Priscilla's aunt from interfering when he wished to have Priscilla to himself. That Duncan had been intrigued with a description of Lady Cordelia and eager to come to Stenborough Park did not alter the fact that he was now in grave condition.

A hand stroked his back. He closed his eyes and savored it, for he recognized Priscilla's gentle touch.

Turning, he raised his hands to bring her into his arms. He paused when he saw she was not alone. Her children were clustered around her. Even so, he might still have pulled her close if her aunt were not lowering herself to a wooden box that had held the costumes he brought.

"Why don't we sit?" Priscilla asked. "Have you heard anything of Duncan's condition?"

"No, not yet, although Dr. Dommel promised me that he would send word as soon as he knew if—" He forced a smile and asked in a near whisper, "How are the children faring?" An inkling of a smile sifted across his lips. "And your aunt?"

"Aunt Cordelia wishes us to leave posthaste," she whispered beneath the rustle of her costume, "but she is anxious to learn how Duncan fares. It appears your matchmaking might have been a success if . . ." She shivered.

He pointed to another box. "Why don't you sit there?" he asked, raising his voice as the children edged nearer, obviously not wanting to be far from their mother.

Priscilla nodded, but she did not move.

"What is wrong?"

"My knees are as stiff as your ruffled collar." She sat without her usual grace.

When Isaac clambered onto the box beside her, Neville picked him up and set him on a pillow lying on the grass. Sitting next to Priscilla, he stretched his legs across the ground toward where Daphne and Leah were pulling pillows forward so they could remain within arm's reach of their mother.

"What happened to Duncan is not your fault, Neville," Priscilla said.

"How did you know what I was thinking?" He leaned his hand behind her.

"I know you."

"Very well, it seems." He sighed. "I appreciate your words, Pris, but they do not ease my guilt."

"You have no time to be guilty. We need to discover who fired those arrows and stop him from using that bow again!"

His eyes widened. "Pris, don't tell me that you plan to go in search of this murderer on your own."

"Of course not. I expect you to help. After all, Duncan is your friend. Does he have any enemies?"

"Most likely. Duncan is pushy, too sure of himself, and unwilling to concede any argument." He smiled. "Quite a bit like me."

Leah giggled. "And like Mama."

Priscilla squeezed her daughter's hand. "And my children."

She looked past her daughters when the flap opened again, sending in some needed cool air. When she saw who stood on the other side, she came to her feet.

Radley Forshaw was only a few years older than Daphne, but the constable from Stonehall-on-Sea was very serious about his position and its duties. His windblown reddish brown hair beneath the cap he was removing revealed how rapidly he had traveled to Stenborough Park.

"Good afternoon, my lady," he said to Aunt Cordelia, then faced them. "Good afternoon, my lady, sir. How is the wounded man?"

"I have not yet heard," Neville replied.

"Do you know his name?" He reached into a pouch he wore on his belt and drew out a bottle of ink and writing materials.

"Duncan McAndrews."

Priscilla sat when she saw the constable's difficulty trying to write while standing. He would not sit while she remained on her feet.

"The facts as I have them so far," the constable said, "are that someone fired a crossbow, and one man was killed in addition to Mr. McAndrews being wounded."

"Crossbow?" gasped Priscilla. "How do you know?"

"The arrow," answered Neville before the constable could. "A quarrel—a crossbow arrow—is different from the arrow used with a longbow."

Priscilla stood, motioning the constable not to leap to his feet. "I believe this is not something the children need to hear."

"But, Mama—"

"Isaac, that is enough." Her voice warned she would not welcome any arguments. "Aunt Cordelia, will you watch over them while we discuss this elsewhere?"

Her aunt nodded.

Tears filled Priscilla's eyes. She had never seen her aunt appear so shaken, not even when Priscilla's father—her aunt's brother—died. Not even when one of her aunt's three late husbands had been buried.

"I will be back as soon as I have news about Mr. McAndrews," Priscilla said. "I promise."

"Thank you." She wrung her hands. "This is unsettling. If that arrow had been a few inches to the right, it could have struck me or one of the children."

Priscilla waited until Neville and Constable Forshaw had emerged from the tent, then walked with them toward the house. All around, Lord Stenborough's guests stared as if they could guess the truth simply by watching the three of them.

They left the area where the tents were pitched and stepped down into a garden with a pool at its center. At other times, Priscilla would have enjoyed lingering to explore the flower beds and see what fish swam in the shallow waters, but not today.

"Have you spoken to others?" asked Neville.

Constable Forshaw nodded.

"What have they said? Did anyone see someone with a crossbow?"

"Nobody saw anything. They were so caught up in the make-believe of the gathering." The constable looked at Priscilla. "Did you see anything that might help?"

"We were on our way to the tables when the first arrow was shot," she replied. "I was thinking only of meeting my children and my aunt."

"You cannot believe Lady Priscilla has anything to do with *this*, can you?" Neville added, his voice again honed. He had never quite forgiven the constable for considering Priscilla a suspect in a murder in the spring.

"No, no!" The constable's face became a brilliant red. "If you thought I did, my lady, I beg your forgiveness."

"I did not think that for a moment," she replied. Putting her hand on Neville's arm as they went to the grand house, she gave him a frown that she hoped he understood meant she did not need him to defend her so vociferously.

When Constable Forshaw opened a door, she paused and looked back at the Faire. It appeared to be deserted, but the troupe's wagons remained. She had half-expected the troupe to vanish. Mayhap they knew it would be better to clear themselves of suspicion before they went on to their next performance—or they might not have anywhere to go, as they had planned to remain here for the length of the Faire.

A footman hurried to meet them. He nodded when they spoke their names and urged them to come with him through the cool passage.

Priscilla entered a room that was small in comparison with the other chambers they had passed. The only sound was the whisper of a breeze slipping its invisible fingers around an open bay window. Wood paneling was stained a dark brown that swallowed every drop of sunshine. Beyond an elegant hearth of carved white marble, a door was closed. No one was waiting, which astonished her, because she had thought others would be eager to speak with Lord Stenborough.

The footman said, "I shall have Lord Stenborough informed you are here." He rushed out, his footfalls vanishing into the silence.

As Priscilla crossed the flowered rug, Neville began pacing in front of the tall windows. He must be more upset than he wanted to show. And so was she!

Constable Forshaw stood in the middle of the room, appraising it. She could not guess what he hoped to discover, then saw a glass case near the hearth. Her first hope that it would contain something to explain what had happened vanished when she realized it contained guns rather than crossbows and quarrels.

Footsteps approached, and Priscilla turned. When she saw Reverend Mr. Kenyon entering the room, she wanted to throw her arms around the vicar from Stonehall-on-Sea and tell him how glad she was that he was here. The short, red-haired man had been given the living of St. Elizabeth's Church in the village after Priscilla's husband had been sent to a bigger church in London. He must have ridden here with the constable.

"I heard . . . I heard . . ." He put his hand to his right side, and she wondered if he had run all the way from the road.

She steered him to a chair and helped him to be seated. "I am glad to see you," she said. "We could use your prayers for Neville's friend, Mr. McAndrews."

"Is he the man killed?" The vicar looked from Neville to the constable, but both seemed lost in their own thoughts.

"No." She explained what had happened.

The vicar sighed. "Thank heavens you are here to help, Lady Priscilla."

"Me?" She was certain she had misheard him. "The only help I can give is to pray Duncan recovers."

"But you helped uncover facts of another unexpected death last spring, my lady." He came to his feet. "Your insight may make the difference now."

When he glanced past her, she saw Neville and the constable were still in deep thought. Bother! She would have appreciated Neville stepping in to remind the vicar that such matters were best left to the constable. If Constable Forshaw wanted her help, he would ask for it.

She said as much to the vicar, and he nodded reluctantly. "I shall go," he said, "and see if I might sit at Mr. McAndrews's bedside." After bidding her a good day, he left.

Priscilla wondered if either Neville or Constable

Forshaw had taken note of his arrival or departure. The constable was peering at items on the tables as if he expected one to jump up and announce the name of the bowman. By the window, Neville was staring out at the field where the Faire had been held. She took a single step, intending to ask him what he was thinking, when Dr. Dommel appeared in the doorway. He was wiping his hands on a bloody cloth, and Priscilla wanted to recoil. She forced herself to be calm as he entered.

"How is Duncan?" Priscilla asked.

"Too early to tell," the doctor answered. "You are—"

"Priscilla Flanders. Is it too early to tell if he will live?"

He patted Priscilla's arm. "Yes. Being able to give you an answer requires a wait of a few hours or mayhap even a few days. You must be patient." His smile broadened as his gaze roved along her in a most unmedical manner.

"I can be patient, doctor." She stepped back. "However, my aunt is deeply concerned. I shall let her know that you will tell us immediately if there is a change in Mr. McAndrews's condition."

"My lady, so many people have inquired and—"

"I would consider it a *personal* favor to have Lady Cordelia told without delay." She did not look at Neville as she put the emphasis on the word "personal," suggesting she was not averse to the doctor's brazen stare. Neville might be frowning or he could be trying not to laugh.

Dr. Dommel smiled and tossed the bloody cloth onto the hearth. She was horrified at the thought he might try to clasp her hand, but he did not. Rather, he said, "I would be a cur not to agree to ease a lady's distress."

Neville's hand on her arm drew her toward a settee covered in dark red satin. "You look a bit unsteady, Pris. I think you should sit and rest, for I fear these tidings have unsettled you more than you realize."

She faced him, about to retort that she did not need to be treated like a fragile figurine. Then he motioned slightly with his head toward the settee, and she understood he was planning something to obtain answers. She wished she had his skill to make half-truths sound honest. He had told her once it was not lying so much as a creative juxtaposition of the facts.

He sat her and whispered, "Try to look faint while I talk with the doctor and our friend Forshaw."

"All right, but—"

"I will share every tidbit with you, but the doctor needs to keep his mind on Duncan rather than on perusing you." He gave her a swift smile. "Dash it, Pris. Why do you have this strange effect on men at the very worst times?" His fingers brushed her cheek; then he went to where the other men were waiting. "Let us speak in the hallway so Lady Priscilla may regain her equilibrium. I am sure you need some quiet, don't you, Pris?"

"That would be nice." She wished she could guess what Neville intended.

She watched the three men leave. Constable Forshaw hesitated to go first, as if he expected one of the others to pull a bow and fire an arrow into *his* back. She rested her elbow on the settee's arm and sighed. Everyone was on edge. Why not? A man was dead and another severely wounded.

Gnawing on her lower lip, she prayed Duncan would not die. Her entreaties were not only for his sake, but for Neville's. He had shown he would never be able to forgive himself for inviting his friend here. Tears pricked her eyes. It was an uncommon and not a pleasant idea that Neville would need protection from his own lofty expectations of himself.

A door at the far side of the room crashed open. Lord Stenborough stormed in and swept the room with a glower. When his gaze settled on Priscilla, his scowl deepened to rut his face. "Where is Hathaway?"

Rising, she looked toward the hall. Constable Forshaw and Neville were in intense conversation with Dr. Dommel. The three slanted toward each other, giving the appearance that they wanted no one else to be privy to what they were saying.

When Lord Stenborough started to stride past her, Priscilla said, "I would not disturb them right now, Lord Stenborough."

"I can—"

"I am sure Constable Forshaw will be anxious to speak to you, as well, once he has finished with Neville and the doctor."

"Constable?" The viscount halted with one foot in the air and an arm outstretched. Slowly he lowered his foot and then his arm before facing her. "The constable is here?"

"Constable Forshaw from Stonehall-on-Sea." Going around the settee, she put her hand on its back. She was amazed how much she appreciated its sturdiness, and she wondered if Neville had sensed something she had refused to acknowledge. Her knees were as weak as a dandelion stem. "You need not worry about incompetence. Constable Forshaw has experience in this sort of crime now."

"I did not know that." He groped for a chair. Grasping it, he stared at her.

"Can I help you?" she asked, looking past him to a woman peering around the door.

"Help me?" gulped Lord Stenborough.

"I—I want to speak to Edwin," the woman said in an uneven voice. She was dressed in a bright blue satin gown embroidered with a fleur-de-lis pattern. Its split skirt revealed many rows of lace. Over her graying hair, she wore an inverted cone with a filmy veil drooping from its tip to flow beneath her chin. Jewelry glittered around her neck and arms and on almost every finger. The outfit, which might have looked charming on a girl Leah's age, seemed bizarre on a woman who must have already entered her fifth decade.

Lord Stenborough whirled and gasped, "Rita! What are you doing here?"

"I was told you were here." Taking a deep breath, she squared her pudgy shoulders and raised several of her chins. "Is this your newest *friend,* Edwin? What happened to you and—?"

"This is Lady Priscilla Flanders. Her friend was hurt. I came to discover how he is doing."

"What kind of lie is that?" The short woman folded her arms over her full bosom. "I have heard too many of your lies. Do you think I would believe such a lame one? I . . ." She stared at the doorway, her mouth becoming a perfect O.

Neville and Constable Forshaw entered and were introduced to Rita, Lord Stenborough's suspicious spouse. As they answered the lady's many questions, Lady Stenborough began to weave.

"Sit down," Priscilla ordered gently, steering the lady to a chair. As she sat Lady Stenborough there, she said, "Something bracing would help right now."

Lord Stenborough nodded. He rang for some brandy to be brought.

Priscilla remained beside Lady Stenborough because she was concerned about the lady—and because the viscountess had a strong grip on Priscilla's hand. Although she wanted to ask Neville what he and the constable had learned from Dr. Dommel, who must have returned to his patient, she knew she had to have patience.

Listening to Constable Forshaw greet Lord Stenborough as if the constable were their host, Priscilla watched Neville. She was not sure why. When his face was emotionless like this, she could not guess what he was thinking. He did not look in her direction as he greeted Lady Stenborough.

Brandy was delivered, and Priscilla poured some for Lady Stenborough. She held out the glass. Lady Stenborough whispered her thanks, refusing to meet her eyes.

Priscilla was vexed when she saw the men had left again. Bother! It was not like Neville to shut her out of such conversations; then she relented. Neville knew—as she did—that neither the constable nor Lord Stenborough would speak plainly if a woman was listening. She had become so accustomed to the conversations she and Lazarus and Neville had shared that she was always frustrated with these situations. It was further proof Neville and her late husband were extraordinary men.

"What are *you* doing here?" Lady Stenborough asked with abrupt venom.

Looking over her shoulder, Priscilla was astounded to see Orysia Aleksandovicheva entering as if she were the lord's wife. Orysia scanned the room, and Priscilla could almost see her adding up the value of the items in it. Lady Stenborough was wise to be concerned about actors being allowed to run tame through her house.

"Pardon me, my lady," Orysia said in a fawning tone, "but I need to speak with you posthaste. I have seen something I must tell you about without delay."

"The constable is in the corridor," Priscilla said.

The fortune-teller shot a withering glance at her, but she wore an expression of concern when her gaze shifted back to the viscountess. "It is not a matter for the constable, but for Lady Stenborough. My lady, may I show you?"

"Yes. Yes." Lady Stenborough put her brandy on a table and leaned forward as Orysia knelt on the carpet.

Priscilla watched in grudging respect as Orysia shuffled the cards she had been carrying. The fortune-teller's hands moved at an eye-blurring speed. The children would enjoy watching this exhibition. Mayhap she would take them to Orysia's tent later in an effort to take their minds from the horror they had witnessed.

"Lady Stenborough," Orysia said as she spread out a pattern of cards, "you must take care."

"What do you see?" the viscountess asked, bending down even farther.

Orysia pointed a long fingernail at one card, then another. "See this? It tells me trouble awaits you if you continue on the path you are traveling. You must seek another path immediately. If you don't . . . " She shivered as she gathered up the cards, holding them between her hands as if the deck needed to be warmed.

This sort of reading was not what she wanted to expose her children to, Priscilla decided. Seeing Lady Stenborough's pale face, she said, "Mayhap your next reading will be more positive . . . and more conclusive. There are many paths we each travel every day."

Orysia came to her feet. "You mistake my meaning, Lady Priscilla. I do not speak of a path across a field or along the sea. I speak of the path of one's life."

"I understood that quite clearly, but I understand as well that the path ahead of us is not as rigid as a path cut into the earth by many feet. Each decision we make has an affect on it."

"True." Her lips curled up into a satisfied smile. "Now you see, as Lady Stenborough does, the importance of my reading. She must make the right decisions so she does not follow the path I have seen."

"Yes. Yes." Lady Stenborough fumbled for her glass and took a deep drink.

Flashing Priscilla a superior smile, Orysia flowed out of the room.

Priscilla sat next to the viscountess. "You must not take such nonsense seriously."

"How do you know it is nonsense?"

"I could shuffle cards and tell you whatever I wanted, too."

Lady Stenborough shook her head. "But you are not a fortune-teller. Orysia Aleksandovicheva is a renowned one."

"She may be famous, but have any of her predictions come true?"

"Many."

"Tell me some, and I will listen."

The viscountess came to her feet. "Why should I try to sway you when you have made up your mind to dismiss her words? I must heed her. I must not follow the path I have been upon, or danger will come for me."

Priscilla stared in disbelief. Somehow, Orysia had induced Lady Stenborough to believe her tales were true. None of this made sense.

Standing, she was about to ask a question when someone burst into the room. Lady Stenborough looked past her, screamed, and swooned, splashing brandy over Priscilla.

Paying it no mind, Priscilla whirled. A young man stood in the doorway. Pain and fear tightened his face. Then the bloody length of his leg caught her eyes.

Crimson pulsed past the young man's fingers as he cried, "I have been shot! They are going to kill us all!"

FIVE

Lady Stenborough roused, jumped to her feet, and swayed. She opened her mouth to scream, but no sound came out.

"Catch her!" Priscilla called as the men raced in.

Neville grabbed the reeling woman, and Constable Forshaw helped him get her back to the chair as Priscilla plucked a cloth off a nearby table. She hoped the embroidered material was not valuable. Pushing past everyone, she went to where the young man was bleeding on the rug.

"Sit down," she said to him as she had to Lady Stenborough.

The blond lad collapsed onto the settee, and she held the towel over the blood coursing down his pumpkin-colored stockings. He winced, biting his lip.

"What is your name?" she asked.

"Burr." He lifted a corner of the material to gaze at the deep gash in his thigh. With a moan, he managed to choke, "John Burr."

She pressed the cloth back on his leg. When another piece was held out to her, she whispered her thanks and took it. She handed it to Burr, then looked up at Neville. She was not surprised to see he was expressionless, but she had no trouble guessing what he was thinking.

"I sent a footman to watch over the children and your aunt," he said as he knelt beside her. Lifting off the cloths to examine Burr's leg, he frowned. "Burr, this does not look as if a ball struck you."

"Not a ball, but an arrow."

"Arrow?" Constable Forshaw peered over Neville's shoulder. "Another arrow? What happened?"

"I was at the castle, where I was supposed to be playing a drum this afternoon, and I . . ." Burr's eyes rolled back in his head as he slumped against the settee, senseless.

Priscilla moved him into a more comfortable position. Constable Forshaw pulled off his coat and crumpled it into a ball to go under the boy's head.

She rose and stepped past Lord Stenborough, who was staring in disbelief. As she had guessed, several servants were in the hallway. She gestured to a young woman.

"Get Dr. Dommel," Priscilla said. "Tell him it is an emergency."

"An emergency?" The maid's face lost all color.

"Tell him another person has been struck by an arrow."

"An arrow? Lor', m'lady! 'Oo would do that?"

Priscilla gave her a shove toward the stairs. "Answers will come after this young man is tended to." She walked back to Lord Stenborough. "My lord, I think it would be for the best if you arranged for Lady Stenborough to be somewhere else while Dr. Dommel tends to this wound."

"Yes. Yes," he mumbled. He stared at Burr and the blood seeping through the cloth.

As she had with the maid, Priscilla gave him a gentle prod. He staggered toward the bottle of brandy. She stepped out of his way and bumped into someone. Not just someone. Neville! Resting her head back against his firm shoulder, she resisted her craving to throw her arms around him. His embrace would shut out the rest of the world and the madness infecting it.

He ran his fingers along her arm. Against her hair, he whispered, "Are you going to be all right here?"

"Alone?"

"I should help Stenborough with his wife."

"He has servants for that."

"I know, but I would like a view of the grounds from an upper floor. It might allow me some clue as to where the arrows were fired from."

Although she wanted to plead with him to stay with her, she nodded. "I will be fine here. Whoever is firing the arrows is outside." She shivered.

"Pris, your aunt will not allow a hair on the head of the fifth earl to be as much as tousled."

She smiled, amazed she could. Aunt Cordelia would be as protective of Daphne and Leah as she was of Isaac, who had inherited his grandfather's title of Lord Emberson. "Go," she murmured. "I will wait here with Burr until Dr. Dommel arrives."

Neville went to where the lady was sprawled on the chair. He slipped his hands beneath Lady Stenborough's shoulders and lifted her. A moan dribbled from her lips and a curse from Neville's.

"Come on, Stenborough," he muttered through gritted teeth. "I could use your help. She is your wife, after all."

Neville's words seemed to startle Lord Stenborough out of his trance. He picked up his wife's silly hat and set it on her stomach, then patted her arm as gingerly as he would a snake.

Priscilla frowned. Lord Stenborough must abhor his wife, for he did not wish to touch her, even now when she was in need of help. She wondered if he had reasons other than her accusations of infidelity—an unfortunately too common situation among the *ton*—to despise her.

Picking up a napkin from the tray beside the brandy bottle, Priscilla wet it with some of the brandy before putting the cloth on Lady Stenborough's head. The woman groaned again, but her eyes stayed closed.

"He is going to kill all of us!" Burr called. "Why aren't you doing something?"

Priscilla went back to where Burr was trying to stand. She put her hands on his shoulders. "Be quiet. The doctor will be here soon."

As if he had been waiting to be announced, Dr. Dommel bustled into the room. He took a quick look at the blood and ordered the room cleared.

She glanced around. Save for Burr and the doctor, she was the only one remaining in the room.

"Don't go, my lady," moaned Burr.

"This is no place for her," Dr. Dommel said in a no-nonsense voice.

"Please!"

Priscilla dampened her arid lips as she imagined her son among strangers, scared and hurt. She would not want someone to ignore his pleas, so she must not abandon this young man.

"Dr. Dommel," she said, "I will not interfere."

"Or swoon."

"I don't swoon. I am made of stronger stuff than that."

The wrong thing to say, because the doctor glanced at her again with a smile that suggested examinations that had nothing to do with being a doctor. "Yes, I can see you are well made in many ways. Your aunt says you do not have callers. Mayhap I might—"

"Dr. Dommel, your patient . . ."

"Yes. Yes." With obvious reluctance, he looked back at Burr. "Now, what happened to you, young man?"

"I was shot! They are going to kill us one by one."

"Calm down," Priscilla said. "It may have been an accident."

"No. No!"

"Let the constable determine that."

"You will ask him to investigate?" Burr seized Priscilla's hand.

"I doubt I could halt him, Burr." She tried to extract her fingers from his before he crushed them. Putting one hand over his, she slipped her fingers away. When she saw the needle Dr. Dommel held, nausea whirled through her stomach. She took Burr's hand again as the doctor began stitching the wound closed.

She wanted to look away, but her eyes seemed to have a mind of their own. They focused on the needle Dr. Dommel was wielding with skill. The sickness in her stomach threatened to rise as Burr moaned.

A hand on her waist broke her mesmerism with the appalling sight. "Come on, Pris," murmured Neville, putting his other hand on her arm and drawing her fingers out of Burr's grip. "We do not need you fainting, too."

She nodded, glad not to speak. With his arm about her, he steered her out of the room. She struggled to control her rebellious stomach as she clutched his velvet sleeve. She let Neville guide her to an uncomfortable bench. Her legs folded, and she sat.

Neville handed her a cup. She took a cautious sip. Just tepid tea. She would have preferred something stronger right now, but she was not sure if she could have swallowed it.

"Thank you," she whispered. Raising her head, she added, "I thought you were going to reconnoiter the grounds from above."

"Lady Stenborough has a very assertive abigail who herded us out in quick order." He chuckled, then sighed. "Are you doing all right now?"

"Better." She set the cup on the bench and stood. "What are you going to do?"

"Stay here until I hear how Duncan's doing."

"I assumed that." She looked along the hallway, wanting to stay and wanting to be certain her children were safe. "And then?"

"I am going to find out who tried to kill him and the lad."

"Dr. Dommel believes Burr was hurt by accident."

"And you believe the good doctor?"

Priscilla faced him. "I have no idea what to believe any longer."

"One thing you must believe." He put his hands on her shoulders. "A murderer has been invited to the Faire."

Priscilla ducked to enter the tent. Before she could do as much as hug her children or reassure her aunt that Duncan was still alive, Daphne gripped her hands and cried, "Mama, is Leah with you?"

"With me? No. Isn't she here?"

Daphne shook her head.

"Aunt Cordelia!" Priscilla cried. "Why didn't you alert me the moment you noticed she was gone?"

"She just found out herself," Daphne said, hurrying to defend her great-aunt, an act that under other circumstances would have pleased Priscilla, for it showed signs of maturity. Now she did not have time to consider that.

Aunt Cordelia wore an expression of chagrin, and Priscilla could not recall ever seeing that emotion on her aunt's countenance. "She must have slipped out when I was speaking with Lady Clanniton."

Priscilla focused her gaze on her children. "What of the two of you? No, never mind. There is no time to debate this now. Do you know where she was going?"

Isaac nodded. "She wanted to retrieve her hair ribbon that she—" Guilt filled his eyes before he stared at his feet. "She lost it when we missed our midday meal." His tone suggested it was as much of a crime to skip a meal as it was for someone to kill the viscount's guests.

"I shall go and bring her back."

"Send someone else, Priscilla," urged her aunt.

"Wait here. I shall not be long. I believe there is some food in the hamper we brought with us. Daphne, look in the basket and prepare servings for six." When her aunt frowned at the idea Neville would be joining them, Priscilla paid her no mind. "If Neville returns before I do, please inform him where I have gone."

Daphne flung her arms around her mother. "Do be careful, Mama."

"I will go with you," Isaac said, raising his chin in

defiance of their unseen enemy. "That is what an earl should do."

"An earl should stay here and safeguard those who need him," Priscilla replied with a smile.

Slipping out of the tent so she did not have to get into a further brangle with her son or her aunt, she hurried toward the Faire buildings, which looked wretched and abandoned. Bother! Leah should have known better than to risk herself for a hair ribbon, especially one her brother had probably tugged out of her hair, if Priscilla had read his conscience-stricken expression correctly.

When she reached the area where the banquet was to have been held, she was not surprised to find it empty. She bent beneath the ropes. A thread snapped, warning that her costume was not meant for such actions. Mayhap she should have changed. No, she had not wanted to spare the time. She had needed to get here before the murderer returned and attacked her daughter.

A form popped out of the shadows, and Priscilla bit back her scream. The young man carried a bucket and some rags. When he looked from her to the blood that marked the spot where Roland had been slain, she knew he was there to erase any signs it had happened.

"Ye should leave," he said. "This be no place fer ye."

"Nor for you." She pointed at the reddened boards. "Constable Forshaw may wish to see that."

"Why?"

"Leave it as it is until you have been told otherwise by Lord Stenborough."

The viscount's name halted the young man. He

nodded, and she knew he did not want to risk the troupe finding more disfavor with their patron.

"Have you seen a young girl?" she asked. "Twelve years old and wearing a yellow costume. She was looking for a hair ribbon."

"I 'ave not seen 'er."

"Can I look around?"

He dampened his lower lip before saying, "It may be dangerous."

"I know, but she is my daughter."

Something crashed, and he jumped, splashing water over his shoes. He raced away.

"Leah?" called Priscilla. "Leah, are you here?"

She got no answer and saw nothing but a few birds pecking at food that had been spilled on the ground. Mayhap Leah had already left, but that made no sense. She would have seen her daughter while walking here. Unless Leah decided to explore what was behind the cloth that served as a backdrop to the king's entrance. Taking a deep breath, she walked toward the cloth, edging around the blood-stains.

She paused when she saw a feather poking between the boards. A purple feather. She picked it up, running her fingers along its slanted edges. This feather had been fletched to fit into an arrow. It must have broken off when Roland's corpse was moved.

But what kind of bird had purple feathers?

She ran her fingers through the trampled grass, looking for anything else. Nothing. Standing, she looked to her left. The Faire's buildings were in front of her. Then she looked in the opposite direction. A clump of bushes. It could have served as a blind for the archer.

Priscilla strode toward the bushes, then faltered. She had not come here to find clues. She needed to find Leah. When she saw Neville or the constable, she would share what she had discovered. Now she needed to find Leah.

"What are you doing here?" demanded a voice behind her. Constable Forshaw!

"Come here and see these briars." She pointed toward the bush. "If you will examine them while I look for—"

Neville grasped her arm. His face was taut with anger. "Priscilla Emberley Flanders, have you lost every ounce of common sense you have?"

She stared, shocked. Never had he addressed her so. Somehow she managed to choke out, "I am looking for Leah."

"She—and her hair ribbon—are safe back at your tent. She skulked back through the water garden, hoping she was not seen. You should not be here."

"She is safe?" She released a heart-deep sigh. "Thank heavens."

"You should not have come here," the constable said. "My lady, you need to trust me to take care of such things."

"I do trust you, Constable Forshaw. However, you and Neville were busy elsewhere." She glanced again at Neville. His fury had not lessened. "Would you have done otherwise?"

Neville loosened his grip on Priscilla's arm. He could not fault her for being determined the children were kept from harm, although he wondered if she had any notion of how his rage came out of fear for *her*. To see her here, so close to where two men had been attacked, he had to fight every instinct that urged him to toss her over his shoulder and get her out of possible danger.

When her lips tilted in a quivering smile, he guessed she was fighting hard not to give in to fear. He would have liked to tell her to take the children and her aunt and return to Mermaid Cottage, but Forshaw had told Stenborough that the guests must remain at Stenborough Park until the constable had the opportunity to speak with each one. Even so, Neville would have ignored the constable's edict and sent Priscilla and the others back to Stonehall-on-Sea . . . if she would have gone willingly without him and Duncan.

Then there was the problem of Stenborough insisting that the Faire continue.

"No," he said in reply to Priscilla's question, "I would not have done otherwise. You were mentioning these briars?"

Her smile steadied as Forshaw scowled. "I found this."

He took the purple feather. His knowledge about arrows and quarrels was limited, but he could recognize this feather had been cut to fit into a shaft. "Where?"

"By where Roland was killed." She shivered, and he knew how unsettled she was even though she was trying to appear serene. He did ponder why she bothered when the rest of them were obviously unnerved.

Save for Stenborough, whose thoughts seemed to be focused on continuing his birthday celebration.

"When I found it," she continued, "I looked in each direction to figure out from where it might have been fired. That is when I noticed these briars."

Neville pricked his fingers as he tried to separate

the snarled branches. He yelped when one stuck hard enough to draw blood. "If someone fired a crossbow from here, he must have been wearing many layers of clothing. All those clothes would have made it difficult for the archer to sneak away without being seen. Maybe the arrows came from somewhere else."

"Where?" asked the constable; then he squared his shoulders. "No need to answer, Sir Neville. I am sure the answer will come clear when I investigate this."

"I would like to be as certain as you are."

"Neville," cautioned Priscilla.

He patted the hand she put on his arm. He had learned how far he could push Forshaw during his last visit to Stonehall-on-Sea, and he would not irritate the constable past reason.

"What have *you* found out?" she asked before he could say more. "Did you find the arrow that struck Burr? It was not in him when he came seeking help."

Forshaw relaxed enough to smile. "It was found by the castle. Near where he was hit."

"It could not have struck him too deeply," Neville added. "The arrow has a serrated tip."

"To hold the target better," she said.

Forshaw pounced on her comment. "I did not know you were such an expert on archery, my lady."

"My father, the late earl, insisted his children learn to use a bow as well as a pistol and a blade. He believed one could never know when one might be in need of such knowledge." Her smile vanished. "It appears he was right."

"Pris, you are quite the renaissance woman." Neville laughed, and Forshaw made a peculiar grumble deep in his throat. He sounded like a dog with a cold.

She started to reply, then gasped, "Did you say *arrow*? Then it was not fired from a crossbow?"

"It is a regular longbow arrow." He frowned. Why hadn't he taken note of that himself? He looked at Forshaw, who was staring openmouthed at her.

"If that is so, we may have two deranged archers," she answered.

"Or one with multiple skills."

Forshaw scowled. "This makes no sense."

"When has murder made sense?" he fired back.

"Neville," Priscilla cautioned again. Bother! Why did Neville have to vex the constable. Constable Forshaw was young and still learning. His eagerness to do his job well should be to his credit.

"Why would someone shoot a lad who works in a troupe that has never been here before?" Neville's eyes widened. "Or have they? I need to speak with the manager posthaste."

"But that does not explain why your friend was a target," Constable Forshaw said.

"Someone is trying to ruin Stenborough's Faire."

"Is that what you think, Sir Neville? You suggested before it might have been an accident."

"Burr had not been shot then. One incident can suggest a certain hypothesis. Two incidents suggest something totally different."

"Such as?"

"Such as," Priscilla interjected, "neither were accidents."

Neville's voice was cold. "I must agree."

"I cannot agree," the constable said, "without proof."

"Then let's find it." She did not wait to see if the men followed, for she knew they would.

The castle loomed above the empty field. She wondered how many wagons had carried the pieces needed to put this together. Looking around, she recalled Burr had said he was going into the castle. So whoever had fired the arrow was not in the faux building.

Turning around, she would have run into the constable and Neville if they had not hastily stepped aside.

"Where are you off to, Pris?" Neville asked.

"One moment." She went to where a length of canvas was half raised, abandoned she guessed, when the guests and entertainers rushed to safety.

Sun-dried red-and-blue-striped canvas was hooked to a pole rising almost ten feet above the ground. The fabric scratched her fingers when she ran them along it. It was a solid piece. No flaps that would have let someone poke a bow out to take aim at Burr.

She saw a shadow that clung to the stripes near the bottom of the tent. She bent. It was a hole, about four inches long. The canvas had been sliced. She guessed with a knife. Jabbing her fingers through it, she shuddered. Four inches long and just wide enough for an arrow to be aimed through.

Standing, she said, "Constable Forshaw, here is your proof that this was not an accident."

SIX

"What?" Constable Forshaw did not like the idea of elbowing aside a lady, especially one who had treated him as kindly as Lady Priscilla had after he had been foolish enough to accuse her once of murder. She had proved him wrong, much to his relief, and she had never rubbed his nose in his mistake. Since then, she had spoken with the leaders in Stonehall-on-Sea about getting him an assistant so he would not be so overworked that he made such errors.

He had accepted the offer of help, not reminding the village council that he had done nothing wrong in considering Lady Priscilla a suspect when the body was found in her garden. The lady had said as much herself. Even Sir Neville had accepted—albeit reluctantly—that Constable Forshaw would have been even more mistaken *not* to count the late parson's wife among the suspects.

That investigation seemed so simple in comparison to this bumble-bath. He wished Stenborough Park and its absurd Faire were in the next shire.

When Lady Priscilla stepped away, he squatted to look at the gash in the canvas.

"As you can see," she said, "here is where the arrow came through."

He stood. "That may be true, but there should be some proof other than a slit that could have been made for dozens of reasons."

"That is true."

He was tempted to preen when he saw the admiration in her eyes. In spite of his accusations, he respected Lady Priscilla, as did his neighbors in Stonehall-on-Sea. Her son might get into too much trouble, but she never blamed anyone but the young earl when he was returned to the house with a warning not to get into trouble again.

That temptation vanished when Sir Neville tugged aside the canvas and peered past it. His strained laugh grated on Constable Forshaw's nerves.

"Here is your proof that the arrow striking Burr was most likely an accident," Sir Neville said.

Pushing past the constable, Priscilla slipped beneath the canvas. She was not sure if she was relieved or disappointed to discover she was standing in the middle of what was set up to be some sort of game field. At the far end, targets balanced against small haystacks. A booth that announced three arrows could be had for a penny was set to her left. A rack with bows and quivers waited beside it.

"*This* is where the arrow that hit Burr must have came from," Neville said.

"But the guests had left the grounds," Constable Forshaw argued.

"The guests are not the only ones here." He motioned to a man walking near the targets. "Birch!"

The large man turned around, and his face became the color of the puffy clouds cluttering the horizon. He hesitated, then walked toward them, trying to smile. "Wot can I do fer ye, sir?"

Priscilla was surprised at Birch's polite tone.

"Do you have a few minutes to talk?" Neville asked in a cheerful tone. "If you are busy—"

"I'm not—" He gulped. "I'm not very busy."

"Did you lose something?"

Several unhealthy shades tinted Birch's wide face, and his hands trembled. Again he struggled to swallow as he glanced at Constable Forshaw. He looked back at Neville before asking, "Can I speak t' ye alone?"

"I think you should say what you have to say in front of all of us."

When Birch looked at her, Priscilla wondered why the large man thought she might help. He could have killed her with that knife. He had been boasting about his prowess with it. If he was as skilled with a crossbow . . .

"Let's walk," Neville said to no one in particular. He strolled toward the small building.

Priscilla followed. When she heard a grumble, she turned to see Constable Forshaw gesturing for Birch to follow. The constable was shorter than the big man by nearly a head, but Birch nodded and lumbered toward her.

Tapping a quiver that held only two arrows, Neville murmured, "There is one missing."

"I ain't the one wot killed Roland!" choked Birch. "I swear that."

"No one said you did."

"I thought . . ." The big man took a shuddering breath. His gaze slid away. "There be an arrow missin', and Roland was killed by an arrow." He looked down at his feet. "So I 'eard."

"By a crossbow arrow."

"A crossbow?" Birch gripped the rack. His shoulders slouched as he shook his head like a slow-witted bull. When he looked up, a hint of color had returned to his cheeks. "I thought you were comin' t' accuse me of . . ."

"Of what?" demanded Constable Forshaw. "Why don't you tell us what you are doing here?"

The story was simple. So simple, in fact, Priscilla was astonished there had not been reports of problems at other places the troupe played. If Lord Stenborough's guests wished to try to hit the bull's-eye to win a trinket, they were to be given a bow, a quiver with three arrows, and a quick lesson on how to use them. She guessed most of the guests had never been any closer to a bow and arrow than reading a novel.

"'Tweren't no problem 'til I noticed one of the red-fletched arrows was missin'," Birch finished.

"Red?" Priscilla asked. "What color are the feathers on the arrow you found, Neville?"

"Red, as red as the blood on Burr."

"Burr?" Birch swore under his breath, then added, "I did nothin' wrong."

"No one said you did, Mr. Birch," Constable Forshaw said.

Birch frowned. "'Oo are you?"

"Constable Forshaw."

Birch grew ashen again.

"I would like to speak with you privately, Mr. Birch," Constable Forshaw said.

Birch gave Neville a pitiful glance for assistance. Neville acted as if he had not seen it and bent to look at the other arrows in the quiver.

Constable Forshaw added, "But I would like a word alone with you first, Lady Priscilla."

"Of course, Constable Forshaw," Priscilla said.

Neville stood as Priscilla moved with the constable

toward the targets. He wondered what Forshaw
wanted to ask her out of his earshot.

"Is 'e goin' t'put me in jail?" whined Birch as he
shuffled the dirt with his toe.

"I have no idea what he plans to do."

"If 'e plans t' say I killed Roland—"

"What are you trying to do? Convince him that
you 'doth protest too much'?"

"Wot?"

"Don't you know your Shakespeare, man? *Hamlet*,
Act Three, Scene Two."

Birch scowled. "I ain't an actor. I don't know wot
ye be talkin' 'bout."

"I am telling you to keep your mouth shut before
you provoke the constable into believing he has a
reason to add you to his list of suspects."

That Birch seemed to understand, because he
nodded.

"Who is in charge of these arrows?" Neville asked.

"Me."

"When did you set them out?"

"I was settin' them 'ere when I 'eard the 'ubbub
from where they were servin' the fancy meal. Went
t' see wot was goin' on. When I got back, the arrow
was gone."

"And a bow?"

He frowned. "Didn't count 'em." He went into the
small building, then peeked out. "They all be 'ere."

Neville wondered why he had thought it would be
as simple as searching the tents and wagons for a
missing bow. Even if it had not been returned, the
archer could have hidden the bow.

He stepped aside when Forshaw walked back,
wearing a determined scowl. A hint of sympathy for
Birch was not enough to keep Neville from going to

where Priscilla waited. He was curious about what Forshaw had to say to her.

"Nothing of import," Priscilla said as soon as he asked.

He drew her hand into the crook of his arm while they walked toward the tents. More people were wandering about the field.

"Vultures," he muttered. "No doubt they have heard how Burr was injured, and they don't want to miss seeing the next person pierced with an arrow."

"Neville, be more forgiving. Everyone is unsettled by an accident." She paused, then said, "Even when it is not an accident."

"I thought you had agreed—"

"Neville, I never thought you would treat me as if I had no brain in my skull."

"I never would."

"Then please refrain from suggesting you wish me to believe that firing at Burr was an accident. A single arrow was fired, and it went through that slit. I find that uncommonly unlikely."

"Or uncommonly unlucky."

Priscilla faced him. "Why are you persisting with this when the truth is right in front of you?"

"Because I can see no reason for why the three victims were targets."

"Yet."

He smiled. "Yet."

"Hathaway!" came a shout from her left.

A tall man, who was leaning on a carved rosewood cane and dressed in a long, fur-lined robe over a blue doublet, strode toward them. He was older than Priscilla had guessed by the speed of steps. As he approached, she saw his face was folded into ridges of wrinkles. Silver brightened his dull brown hair. His eyes twinkled even more brightly as he grasped Neville's hand and pumped it as if trying to test if his arm would bounce out of his shoulder.

"What in hell—" The man glanced at Priscilla, then amended, "What are you doing here, Hathaway? Could it be you are looking for work?"

"Would you hire me, Bennett?" Neville chuckled and clasped the older man's arm.

Priscilla appraised the man anew as Neville introduced him as Albert Bennett, the manager of the troupe. When the two men spoke of people they knew, she listened quietly. This was a part of Neville's life he seldom mentioned, unlike the years when he had been involved with crime—either as a thieftaker with Bow Street or as a thief himself. No one seemed to know which. If she asked, she was unsure if he would tell her the truth, for he enjoyed creating a tale better suited for the stage than a conversation.

"We have been presenting this show," Mr. Bennett said, with a smile in her direction, "for more than a year. Before that, we portrayed characters from various nations on the Continent. It was a simple transition when we received requests to create the Middle Ages and a market day and Faire."

"That confirms my suspicions." Neville chuckled. "I doubted Stenborough has the imagination to devise this on his own."

"He hired us after seeing us in Norfolk earlier in the summer. I regret saying yes."

Priscilla asked quietly, "So you have not had any trouble previous to this?"

"Nothing like this." Mr. Bennett ran his fingers through his graying hair. "Times are never easy when one is surrounded by actors."

"The creative temperament?"

Neville raised a brow. "Rather, you should say the drinking and not caring what impression one leaves behind when one is traveling from place to place. No insult to you, Bennett."

"None taken." Mr. Bennett's smile returned. "If I were not aware of what mischief actors can find, I would not still be in this business. A good manager needs to keep ahead of them, always anticipating where they might find trouble before the thought even enters their minds."

"But you never imagined murder."

"No, never."

Priscilla could not mistake the dismay and disquiet in Mr. Bennett's voice. "Have these actors been with you for a long time?"

"Yes. Most have been with the troupe for more than a year."

"And the others?"

"Several of the dancers have been with us for only a few months. The woman who tells people about their futures—"

"Orysia?" she prompted.

"Yes, Orysia whatever-her-long-last-name-is joined us about six months ago. She had been working in London before that, so I hired her. Not many actors wish to come out into grassville when they can earn a steadier living in town."

"So why did she?" Priscilla asked.

Neville smiled as Mr. Bennett shrugged. "Pris, people in the theater don't ask such questions. It is understood that, unless someone offers information, nobody pries into someone else's background."

"Which allows a convenient haven for a murderer."

Mr. Bennett choked out, "Are you saying one of my actors killed Roland and tried to kill two others?"

"I am saying," Priscilla replied, "it is possible. Your troupe has access to the weapons."

"But they would not do such a thing!"

"How can you know that for certain if you don't know anything about their pasts?"

Neville put his hand on her arm. "Pris, allow me."

She was going to protest, but when she saw his taut face, she nodded. Mr. Bennett was his friend, and Neville would know the best way to obtain information from him. Taking a deep breath, she told herself not to panic. Her children had been close to Duncan when he was shot, but now they were safe with her aunt.

"Bennett," he said, "tell me. Did your king have any enemies in the troupe?"

"Roland was liked by everyone." He sighed and combed his fingers through his hair again. "If it had been some of the others, I would have been able to give you names. Not Roland."

"When do your performers use crossbows?"

"They were supposed to practice this evening, for an exhibition in the morning."

"Where would they have practiced?"

"At the back of the field."

"That is on the opposite side of the Faire from the dining area."

"Yes."

"And you still believe it was an accident?" Priscilla asked.

"An accident?" Lord Stenborough pushed past Neville, surprising her. She had been so intent on Mr. Bennett's answers, she had not heard the viscount approach. With him was a young woman. The redhead was not his daughter, but young enough to be. "Is that what you believe it was? What a relief! That means the Faire can continue."

"I do *not* believe it was an accident!" she retorted. "Lord Stenborough, you should bring this Faire to an end posthaste."

He shook his head. "If there is a murderer about, sending my guests along lonely roads when they will not reach their homes before nightfall might mean more people getting hurt or killed."

Priscilla did not want to agree with him, but he was right. Here, at Stenborough Park, the guests could be brought within the walls of the house tonight. On the morrow, they could take their leave.

"And," he continued, "my birthday celebration is not over."

She looked away, not wanting him to see her fury. Getting into a brangle would not help Duncan or find the one who had shot him. She looked at the woman dressed in the finest fashion standing to Lord Stenborough's right. Her features were even and her eyes the brightest blue Priscilla had ever seen. Hair so pale it almost denied being any color curled beneath a stylish bonnet.

"This is Miss Jessamyn Young." Lord Stenborough smiled. "Allow me to introduce Lady Priscilla Flanders and Sir Neville Hathaway."

The young woman dimpled. "It is a pleasure to meet you."

Neville bowed over her hand, and Priscilla offered a greeting. Before either could say or do anything else, Miss Young said, "This whole Faire is wondrous, don't you think? I wish those incidents had not created such a pall over our day."

Lord Stenborough hurried her away. He called

back some excuse whose words Priscilla did not catch.

"Miss Young. Young . . ." mused Neville as Mr. Bennett also took his leave. Chuckling, he said in his customary voice, "'Tis rumored Stenborough likes them young, so she is perfect for him."

"Neville, curb your suppositions. He might be a friend of her father's."

"A situation that will change if Stenborough completes the seduction on his mind. Don't tell me that you failed to take note of how he regarded her, Pris."

"Of course not," she retorted, not willing to own that she had.

He draped an arm around her shoulders and gave her a leer. "Like that."

"I suspect the young lady would have raced away if he chanced to wear such an expression in her company."

"And will you run away, too, Pris?" He looped his finger through her hair.

"Most assuredly. If our host were to look at me like that, nobody could keep me here." She laughed. "You need not have any worries on my behalf because of Lord Stenborough."

His smile faded. "Simply because of the doctor."

"Do not act like a jealous suitor, Neville." She slapped his arm lightly. "It is a role you do not wear well."

"Mayhap because it is no role, but the truth."

She saw sincerity in his eyes. Sincerity and a passion that invited her to toss aside all care and indulge in an adventure made for the two of them.

Stroking his rough cheek, she whispered, "Neville, I—"

"Lady Priscilla! Is that you?"

Priscilla looked over her shoulder and grimaced as Orysia rushed toward them, the scarf on her head flapping like the flags atop the fake castle.

"Thank goodness!" Orysia gasped. "Finally someone who might know something. The constable is as tight-lipped as a first kiss, and no one in the troupe seems to know anything. How is the man who was injured?"

"I don't know."

"Oh, my!" She pressed her hands to her chest, then flung them out in a vain attempt to grasp Priscilla's. When Priscilla kept her hands behind her, Orysia turned to Neville. "Is he going to die?"

He clasped his hands in back of him as well. "We are hoping Dr. Dommel is as interested in saving his life as he is in Lady Priscilla."

"As interested as . . ." Orysia scowled for a moment, then rubbed her hands together. The fortune-teller's skin appeared rough, as if she had done work far more strenuous than pretending to read cards. "Do let me know when he is doing better." She closed her eyes, and her shoulders sagged in a dramatic pose as the coins on her scarf clinked against one another. "I should have seen this. Why didn't I see this?"

Priscilla was tempted to reply that the question was easy to answer. Orysia was not a real seer, but an actress portraying one. Instead, she said, "Mayhap you have seen other things that would be of interest to the constable."

"Me? Why would I know anything about what happened?"

"You are an intelligent woman." She smiled. "I doubt much escapes your notice."

Orysia preened, her smile aimed at Neville. She

was, Priscilla decided, a coquette. "You are right, but I saw nothing, even when I went to the banquet area."

"Did you pick up anything?"

"Nothing of import, I am afraid. Just some items left behind by the troupe. If I had found something important, you can be certain I would have alerted Mr. Bennett or Lord Stenborough." Her smile softened. "Or mayhap you, *Sir* Neville."

"If you see anything else unusual, do let me know, *Miss* Orysia," Neville replied in a sugary tone. Priscilla had to look away before Orysia saw her grin. When Neville took on that tone, wise folks knew to be wary. He might be jesting or he might be serious; either way, he was sure to be in the midst of the uproar that invariably followed soon after.

He edged closer to the actress, who regarded him with a smile. "You will let me know, won't you? No matter the hour of the day or night."

"Of course, *Sir* Neville," she purred. Priscilla would not have been surprised if Orysia had rubbed against him like a cat. "Anytime. Day . . . or night."

"Good." His smile suggested their negotiations were complete and the assignation would come in short order. In a gruffer voice, he said, "Pris, I think I need something cool to drink."

Orysia turned to Priscilla, her expression revealing the actress had become so bewitched by Neville that she had forgotten anyone else stood nearby. Without a hint of shame at flirting so boldly, Orysia said, "Let me know when the doctor is sure Mr. McAndrews is going to live, please. I want to express personally how sorry I am that I did not warn him."

"He does not like sympathy," Neville replied.

"Please let me know."

Afraid that Orysia would not stop begging until one of them agreed, Priscilla said, "Yes, I will."

"Oh, thank you."

"We have to go," Neville added.

"Go. Go!" She fluttered her hands and turned away, her scarf dancing about her. "I will let you know if I learn anything."

"Immediately," he called back.

Priscilla linked her arm with his and tugged him toward the tents. "Enough, Neville. Even a woman who has somehow convinced herself she can see the future will know you are bamboozling her if you don't stop this silliness."

"Silliness? How do you know I did not mean what I said?"

Pausing, she tapped her foot against the ground. "I find it odd that you can speak of your distress with Dr. Dommel offering me solace but you believe I should witness such a flirtation."

"Now *you* sound like a jealous lover, Pris."

"Your ears are bamboozling you as surely as you were Orysia."

"That may be true." He pressed something into her hand and closed her fingers over it. "Keep this for me."

"What is it?" She uncurled her fingers and gasped as she stared at a purple feather. "I thought you gave this to Constable Forshaw."

"That one. I got this from Orysia." He smiled grimly. "I am not an unskilled pickpocket, you know. Come along."

Priscilla tried to match his steps, but he was striding so quickly she needed to move at a near run. "Where did she get this?"

"You heard her." He looked back and chuckled. "Or were you too overcome with jealousy?"

"Do not be absurd."

He slowed so she could catch up as they reached the castle again. "She went to the banquet area where she must have found the feather along with a few pieces of ribbon and lace." He drew them from beneath his coat. "She obviously considers them of no import."

"Which should show you how good an ally she will be."

"Sometimes an unwitting ally can be the very best kind." Before she could answer, he raised his voice and called, "Bennett, a word with you!"

The manager of the troupe left the two young men he was talking with and came over to ask, "What is it?"

Neville took the feather Priscilla held. "Do you recognize this?"

"Mayhap." Mr. Bennett examined it.

"Mayhap?"

"We have quarrels with feathers of this color."

Priscilla glanced at Neville and saw his eyes were narrowed. He was assessing not only what the manager said, but how he said it. In the calmest voice she could manage she asked, "Who uses them?"

"We have had what we call an exhibition between an actor playing Robin Hood and those pretending to be the Sheriff of Nottingham's men."

"Who uses the purple-fletched arrows?" She held out her hand, and he placed the feather on her palm.

"Robin Hood."

"And who is your Robin Hood?"

For a long minute, he was silent. "Usually we invite

someone to join us in the role of Robin Hood as well as participate in the tournament and lead the procession at the Faire's end. Here it was going to be Garvin Harmsworth."

"Lord Stenborough's estate manager?"

"One and the same," Neville said with a rigid smile.

She looked from him to Mr. Bennett's worried face. "But why would Mr. Harmsworth want to shoot anyone?"

"That, my dear Pris, is what I intend to find out."

SEVEN

Upon entering the rooms she had been brought to by a footman, Priscilla was astonished to see her aunt sitting by the window. She ignored the lovely dark green draperies and pale gold walls as she rushed to kneel next to her aunt. Seeing Aunt Cordelia so withdrawn upset her more than she could have guessed. So many times she had hoped her aunt would curb her tongue, but not like this.

"Aunt Cordelia, it will be all right," she said, putting her hand over her aunt's, which quivered with distress.

"Please leave me alone, Priscilla."

"But, Aunt Cordelia—"

"Please leave me alone, Priscilla."

As she came to her feet, Priscilla saw her younger daughter motioning to her frantically from a doorway into another room. She hurried to Leah, glancing back several times at her aunt, who continued to stare out the window. Even when a flash of lightning came through it, Aunt Cordelia did not react.

"She has been like that since we came here," Leah said as soon as Priscilla entered what appeared to be an antechamber to the grand bedchamber beyond it. Perched on the very edge of a green-tufted bench, she rubbed her fingers in her gown, wrinkling it over her lap. "Mama, Daphne and I tried to comfort her, but she sent us away just as she has you."

Before Priscilla could reply, her son threw his arms around her. She was astonished when he asked, "Mama, now that we are in the house, may I visit the dungeon?"

"Not now, Isaac. First we must consider other things."

"But, Mama—"

"Before we leave, I shall speak with Lord Stenborough about giving you a tour of the cellars, where I suspect there are just bottles of wine and dust." She tousled her son's hair. When he grimaced at the action he considered too childish for a boy of his advanced years, she wanted to hug him. His commonplace reaction was the reassurance she needed when everything was bizarre.

He grinned and picked up a glass from a tray holding a pitcher of lemonade. "Not according to—"

Daphne burst in. "Mama, how are you? How is Uncle Neville? How is his friend?"

At the mention of Neville's name, the other children looked up fearfully. She soothed their fears by telling them that Neville had returned to the house with her and that the doctor would alert them as soon as Duncan's situation was stable. When she added that the vicar was with him, they released low sighs of relief.

Priscilla took a cup of lemonade from Daphne and thanked her.

"Do you think the doctor will forget to inform us?" her oldest asked.

"No." She tried to force the image of Dr. Dommel's smile from her head. It had told her what the cost of any personal favor would be. If he tried to collect on that debt in an inappropriate way, she would set him to rights in short order. "I am going to speak with Aunt Cordelia."

"She will not talk with you," warned Leah.

"That is yet to be seen. I can be as mulish as she is."

Thunder heralded Priscilla as she walked back out into the main room of the suite that was as large as the ground floor of Mermaid Cottage. She edged between Aunt Cordelia and the window. More lightning flickered, and she drew a chair next to her aunt's.

"You cannot intend to remain here for the rest of the Faire," Priscilla said.

"I asked you to let me be."

"You did, but you know how seldom I heed you, Aunt Cordelia."

Her aunt's gaze focused on her. "*That* is true. If you had heeded me, you would not have accepted an invitation from *that man*—"

Priscilla translated *that man* into Neville.

"And we would not be here," her aunt continued.

"You should try to like Neville."

"No, for he will give your children wrong ideas." She frowned. "As he gives you. I spoke of my concerns to that pleasant Dr. Dommel, and he seems to share them."

Priscilla kept herself from shaking her head in despair. Dr. Dommel might be pleasant to her aunt, but he was bothersome to her. This, however, was not the time to get into an argument with her aunt.

"You have expressed yourself on that subject many times, but you never have reacted like this. Usually you let everyone—including Neville—know your opinions. Why are you sitting here like a statue? It is not at all like you."

Aunt Cordelia's eyes closed, then slowly opened as thunder crackled overhead, muffled by the thick stone walls. "I saw Mr. McAndrews hit by that arrow, Priscilla."

"You did? You and the children saw it?"

She shook her head. "No, the children did not see. They were too busy arguing about which one of them should sit in which chair. Really, Priscilla," she said, her voice resuming its usual lecturing tone, "I would have thought you had taught them how to deport themselves in public."

"I shall speak to them of it."

"See that you do."

"I am glad they did not see what happened."

Aunt Cordelia seemed to shrink within herself. "So am I! I wish I had not seen it. If I had not insisted we select seats on that side of the table so we would not have our faces to the sun, Mr. McAndrews might not be dying."

Again Priscilla knelt by her aunt. Grasping her hand, she said in the stern voice she used when she wanted the children's attention, "Aunt Cordelia, you must disabuse yourself of the notion *you* did anything wrong. Duncan might not have been the target. After all, another quarrel was fired and struck the man playing the king."

"But if I had not insisted on us sitting there—"

"There is no way to know who might have been injured if you had chosen other seats; that is true. But it is not your fault, Aunt Cordelia. 'Tis the blame of the one who fired the crossbow."

Her aunt did not answer for several minutes, then so abruptly set herself on her feet that she almost knocked Priscilla aside. Looking down, she said, "I believe you are correct *this time.*"

"Thank you." Priscilla stood. That her aunt was unwilling to set aside her belief that Priscilla was incapable of teaching the next earl his obligations was proof that Aunt Cordelia was shaking off her distress.

"I shall seek out that kind Dr. Dommel and discover what he can tell me about Mr. McAndrews."

"He has kept his tongue firmly between his teeth on Duncan's condition."

She thought her aunt would fire back an argument, but instead Aunt Cordelia smiled. "Dr. Dommel is an excellent doctor and a very caring man. Even in the midst of the horror, I could not keep from noticing how kind he was to you, Priscilla."

"He was very kind to all of us."

"But especially to you, my dear."

Could her aunt be trying to do some matchmaking in the midst of this disaster? She knew her aunt too well to dismiss that as silly. Aunt Cordelia wished to see her settled in another marriage, although Priscilla was startled her aunt was discussing a doctor. Her aunt had believed marrying a clergyman was beneath an earl's daughter, so why was she speaking so of a doctor?

That was a question Priscilla could not ask. Nor did she want to hear the answer. Instead, she waited until her aunt had left, then went to join her children. She had let too many other things draw her away from them during this appalling afternoon.

Neville ducked beneath a tree and grimaced when drops splashed from the leaves. The storm had been quick, but left behind a soaked field beneath the gray sky. That did not seem to dampen the fun that had resumed.

He pulled his coat collar higher, glad he had changed back into his customary clothes. This dark blue coat would not be ruined by the rain, for he had worn it many times in London drizzle. His buckskin breeches were spotted with rain. Those silly costumes were fine for a short time, but he was glad to have on boots that did not leak.

When he had learned Stenborough was insisting the entertainment begin anew as if nothing had happened, he told himself he should not be surprised. Stenborough had made no effort to hide his determination to celebrate his birthday and the quarter day exactly as he had planned. No murder, attempted murders, or thunderstorm would halt it.

The fool!

Even the actors, who usually believed the show must continue under any circumstances, were uneasy. One wagon had left, the family who called it home deciding they would rather take their chances on finding work somewhere else. Others had threatened to go, but Bennett had cajoled them into staying.

Neville walked across the flattened grass past the area where jugglers were repeating the routine they had performed in the morning. Now, however, they dropped the clubs and balls frequently. Calls from the hawkers were muted as they bent to whisper with each other, and jokes by the Faire's players seemed strained. Or mayhap it was just his ears. He saw tearstains on one young lass's face before she averted it, and he knew the troupe was proving what good actors they were. Fear lurked nearby, like the storm that had risen up out of the sea.

Where was Bennett? Someone had said Neville

could find the manager near the location where lemonade was being served. Where was that?

Neville cursed when he was nearly jostled off his feet. He turned to discover a young woman in a brocade dress trying to keep the dishes on her tray from crashing to the ground. He steadied them, and she gave him a tremulous smile.

"Pardon me, sir . . . my lord. . . ."

"Sir Neville will do."

She dipped in a curtsy. "Thank you, Sir Neville."

"Can you tell me something?"

"Of course."

"Wasn't the lemonade table right here?" He pointed to the wall of canvas.

"It was moved to the village green."

"Village green?" He could not remember seeing anything that resembled a village green.

The young woman laughed. "Actually, 'tis the village *brown*. With all these fine folks tramping over it, I doubt if a sprig of grass still lives there."

Thanking her, Neville pushed through the crowd that seemed as resolved as Lord Stenborough to make up for the lost hours of merriment. He was unsure if his feet were stepped on more than he was treading on others'. When he heard musicians, he understood why the guests were gathered here. He turned about to try another route.

"*Sir* Neville, how are you?"

He looked to his left to see Orysia standing in front of her garish tent. She waved for him to come closer. In spite of his curiosity about what Bennett had to say, his interest was piqued by Orysia, who wore a fake mole that had not been there when he had last seen her.

Neville asked as he stepped beneath the tent's awning, "Have you seen Bennett?"

"No." She shrugged. "Of course, I have not been looking for him."

"Then what have you been watching for?"

"Watching for?"

"You are standing guard on your tent." Neville waited for her reaction. This woman was too often observing others. A skill she needed for her work, he was ready to own, but he wondered if there was more to her curiosity than that.

Orysia grimaced. "If you wish the truth, *Sir* Neville, I was watching for you or Lady Priscilla. I am worried about you."

"About me or Priscilla?"

"Either." Her lips tilted in a knowing smile that he suspected unnerved those who came to have their fortunes told. It was wasted on him, but he would not tell her that.

"Why are you worried about us?"

"You are his friend."

"Whose friend?"

"The man who was shot."

"Did you see something in your cards to tell you danger is looming for us?"

"You should not belittle what you do not understand."

Do not believe, Neville corrected silently. Smiling, he said, "I meant no insult to you."

She took a shuddering breath. "You are in jeopardy. Everything points to that."

"What everything?"

"My cards." She grabbed his right hand and jabbed at his palm with a long nail. "Look. Right here. There is danger written all over your palm. Come in and let me read for you."

He pulled his hand away. "I need to talk to your boss. Can we do this some other time?"

"All right." As he started to walk away, she added, "If you have any other time left."

Gooseflesh raised along his arms. He shook it off. Orysia was no more able to guess what was going to happen than he was. By Jove, she was good in her role.

Neville followed the music around the corner of the castle. He did not find any lemonade, but he saw Burr working as if nothing had happened.

"You look better," Neville said as the young man put his brush down into a bucket of paint.

"Thanks to the doctor and Lord Stenborough."

"Lord Stenborough?" He laughed when Burr pointed toward a bottle of wine nestled in the grass. Although it was probably not one of the viscount's best, the wine was certain to be finer than anything Burr had ever had. "Have you seen Bennett?"

"He was near his wagon. Talking with that pretty lady who helped tend my leg."

"Priscilla?"

Burr swayed as he bent to pick up his brush again, and Neville wondered how many bottles the young man had enjoyed before this one. "Lady Priscilla? That sounds right. Pretty lady with blond hair."

"Thank you." He started to slap Burr on the shoulder, but stopped himself, suspecting he would send Burr careening into whatever he was painting on the board.

Neville headed for the performers' wagons. What in the blazes was Priscilla doing out here alone? She should know better. He heard his name called and was about to ignore it when he realized two steps later that it had been Priscilla's voice.

Whirling, he went to where she was standing about halfway between the fake castle and the wagons. "What are you doing out here?"

"When did you find time to change?" She looked down at her costume, which flattered her slender form.

"Don't worry about that now."

"No?" She lifted one side of her skirt out of the grass to reveal a line of mud. "I would much rather have my sensible clothes and my high-lows. Mayhap I should change, as well."

"Before you do, I have a question for you. Have you lost your mind?"

"Not that I know of." She smiled. "Of course, if I had lost it, I most likely would be unaware of that fact, wouldn't I?"

"What is wrong, Pris?" He searched her face and saw the unfamiliar lines of strain. "I know you too well not to know that you take on that jesting tone only when you are too upset to speak what is really wrong. Is it Duncan?"

"He is much the same."

"So why are you here instead of within the house where you and the children will be safe?"

Priscilla met Neville's gaze evenly. "How do you know we are safer inside? There are more people outside, so we could be ambushed in the house."

"So where are the children?"

She smiled in spite of herself. "You are the most bothersome man I have ever met, Neville Hathaway! You know quite well they are in the house where I expect they will remain safe."

"With your aunt?"

"Yes. Only a beef-head would dare challenge her now that she has shaken off her first bout of despair at being the reason Duncan was hurt." She hastened to explain, blinking back tears as she thought of her resilient aunt being so distressed.

He stroked her cheek, running his thumb along her jaw. His voice softened. "But, Pris, why are *you* out here where you know dashed well it could be dangerous?"

"I want you to try something with me."

"Really?" His brows rose lecherously.

Although she chided him, she was grateful for his teasing. It, like Isaac's reaction to her tousling his hair, was an affirmation that everything might once again be as it should. "You would be wise to consider if your mind is where it should be," she replied.

"We are in the midst of the Middle Ages, Pris. A very bawdy time when a titled gentleman would not hesitate to seize a woman he wanted and do this." He kissed her swiftly.

Too swiftly, because she wanted to lose herself in his mouth's slow, gentle, demanding caress. When he smiled, she knew he was right not to tempt either of them with that luscious kiss just now. Mayhap later . . .

"Forshaw told me," Neville said, "that he is baffled by the whole of this."

"As are all of us."

"He has been most interested in opinions I have on the matter."

She nodded. "You do know some of the actors in this troupe."

"That is what he is most interested in."

Pausing, she faced him. "Neville, please tell me that he does not believe you are involved."

He wagged a finger in front of her face. "Shame on

you, Pris! Don't you know you should suspect every-one?"

"If it makes you feel better, I could suspect you are mixed up in this somehow."

"Thanks."

"Do not pout, Neville. It is not becoming on a man of your age."

"Thanks again. Now I am suspicious *and* old."

"Not so suspicious." She laughed when he gri-maced; then she grew serious. "I cannot imagine any reason why the constable would believe you might want to kill somebody here."

"Forshaw hinted it might be an old lover's quarrel."

"Be serious!"

"I am, and so is Forshaw, for he is grasping at any idea to stop the murderer before someone else dies. He was hinting that I was jealous of you showing at-tention to Duncan."

Priscilla frowned. "That is absurd. I will tell him so when next I see him."

"Do you really want to help me?"

"How?"

"Forshaw's questions have gotten me curious. I want to try a little experiment, and I want you to help me."

"With what?"

"This." He drew her around a tall wall and pointed to a rack of crossbows.

Every slot was filled. Whoever had planned this murder had left no sign which weapon had been used. Looking at a half-dozen quivers holding quar-rels, tip upward, she saw each one contained four. Four red, four white, four green . . . and four purple. Nothing was missing.

"They even look dangerous," Priscilla said.

Neville withdrew a crossbow from the rack. "Such a weapon would have been comforting when facing a line of mounted knights in armor."

When he handed her one of the quivers, she slung it over her shoulder and followed him down a steeply sloping bank toward a lake visible through the trees. The high grass, damp from the quick storm, tickled her legs as she pushed after him.

Music and voices from the Faire drifted to them on the indolent breeze. Taking a deep breath of the aroma of cooking food, Priscilla wondered if anyone would be willing to sit at one of those tables to eat this evening.

Neville lowered one end of the crossbow to the ground. Setting his foot in a metal stirrup, he held out his hand. She handed him a square-tipped quarrel. He put it in place and pulled upward on the string. It popped from his hand as he was drawing it taut. The arrow flopped to the ground.

"Do not laugh," he warned between gritted teeth as he began again. "This would be easier if I had proper equipment. Archers who use crossbows wear a hook on their belts that goes under the string. When they stand, it pulls the string into place."

"How do you know that?"

He gave her one of those mysterious smiles that whetted her curiosity as he replied, "I have some experience with these."

"In the theater?"

"Not exactly, although I was acting a role at the time." He motioned her back. "Stay away in case the quarrel goes where it should not."

She watched as he tugged again. Sweat jeweled his forehead when he lifted the loaded weapon. With a shiver, she said, "I would not want to face one of those even if I had the heaviest armor in history."

"There are advantages to this century." He balanced the crossbow on his arm. "Such as an understanding of a quarrel's trajectory. I suspect the quarrels fired into the banquet area came from just about here."

"This far?"

"Even an amateur bowman can shoot a crossbow more than a hundred yards."

He raised the crossbow and sighted it. The quarrel sped from it so fast she could only gasp as it hit a tree with a distant thud. That was far more than a hundred yards from where they stood.

When he had fit another quarrel into the bow, he asked, "Do you want to try?"

"Why?"

"I want to see if someone your size could fire it."

She gingerly took the heavy weapon. "Mayhap you should have seen if someone my size could load it first."

"One problem at a time. Go ahead."

Balancing the crossbow against her shoulder, she tried to aim it at the tree he had hit. "I don't think I can hold it steady long enough to fire it."

"Kneel down. I have seen pictures of archers firing like that."

Leaning the bow against the ground, she knelt and took a deep breath. The wet grass soaked her dress and tickled her nose. As she raised the bow, she realized how easily someone dressed in green could have hidden here.

"Put your left hand under the stock," he said as he helped her balance it. "Your right index finger goes on the trigger."

She took a deep breath and aimed the quarrel at

the distant trees. She contracted the trigger, and the string snapped forward. The quarrel sped across the meadow. She rubbed her shoulder and stood. There had not been a recoil as with a pistol, but a twang had reverberated along her arm. She stared at the shaft, which had struck a tree several feet from where she had aimed.

"It is not easy to shoot accurately," she said.

"Mayhap a good eye was not needed."

"Are you saying that anyone among the guests or the troupe or even someone else could have stolen a crossbow and used it?"

Taking the heavy bow from her, he leaned it atop his shoulder and nodded. "That is exactly what I am saying. It makes the whole situation a lot muddier."

Priscilla did not want to agree, although she knew he was right. She walked across the field and tried to tug the quarrel she had shot from the tree. Propping one foot against the trunk, she jerked on it. She yelped when her fingers were scorched as they slid from the shaft.

Handing her the quiver, Neville reached past her and jerked the arrow out of the tree. He went to get the other one and dropped it into the quiver. "I wish I could have given you an answer instead of raising more questions, Pris."

"I did not expect you to have answers." She put the quiver on her shoulder again as they walked back toward the Faire. "I had hoped you might, I have to own."

"We can leave now, if you wish, Pris."

"Leave? Stenborough Park? When your friend is still senseless?"

He sighed. "There is that, but Duncan would not want you to be in danger."

"Let's wait until the morning. Then, if we know something more about Duncan's condition, I can decide what to do."

"You are not thinking of staying longer, are you?"

She set the quiver on its rack. "I wish I could give you an answer to that."

Dropping the crossbow next to it, he grasped her shoulders. "Pris, I know you hate to leave puzzles unsolved, but you need to consider your safety and the safety of your children."

"I have not thought of much else." She slipped from beneath his hands and continued toward the Faire. "That is why I want to get an answer. I do not want this murderer following us to Stonehall-on-Sea."

He raised his voice to be heard over some shouts from their left. "I understand, but you have to consider—" He cursed.

Priscilla turned to follow his narrowed eyes. At a table by the castle wall, two men were arguing. They jumped to their feet.

Something flashed in the sunshine. A dagger!

A woman screamed.

Neville leaped toward them, calling, "Stay back, Pris!"

Her knuckles bleached as she clasped her hands. Neville jumped between the men and shoved them apart. He reached for the blade. It slashed at him. Blood splattered. The knife rose again. He careened backward, crashing into Priscilla. She never saw what struck her head before everything vanished into darkness.

EIGHT

The slap was gentle, but it hurt. Priscilla opened her eyes and stared up at Garvin Harmsworth. The estate manager's smooth smile was firmly in place, but as her eyes focused, she noticed lines of tension edging his mouth.

"How do you feel, Lady Priscilla?" he asked.

"Fine." That was a lie, but she could endure the ache along the back of her head. "What happened?"

Instead of answering, he asked, "Can you sit?"

"Yes.

"Do you need help?"

She shook her head, then wished she had not. Sitting up, she clamped her lips closed. Bother! She was not so squeamish that she fainted at the sight of a dagger. Fainted? No, she had not fainted. She had been knocked into the wall by . . .

"Neville!" she cried. "How is Neville?"

"He is—"

"Pris," Neville said before Mr. Harmsworth could add more, "I am fine."

Something dripped on her hand. She stared at the blood streaming through Neville's fingers, which were clamped to his left shoulder. His face was sickly gray as his pain-thinned lips drew back in a caricature of a smile.

She came to her feet with Mr. Harmsworth's help. "You look as if you are ready to swoon."

"I will be fine." He lurched to the table where the fight had begun. He sat heavily.

"You need to be honest, Neville, when everyone can see you are lying." She ignored the twinge of guilt at chiding him when she had told the same falsehood. "Mr. Harmsworth, please send for Dr. Dommel."

"Yes, my lady." The estate manager rushed toward the house.

"Thanks, Pris," Neville murmured. "I regret giving you an excuse to have to put up with Dommel's lascivious looks again."

"Nonsense." She struggled to keep her tone light as she stared at the blood on his coat and dripping onto the front of his shirt.

"Your aunt wants to make a match for you and the good doctor."

"She cannot be serious about a match with a doctor. Don't be silly."

"Me?" His teasing tone was laced with pain. "Lady Cordelia has found what she believes to be the perfect method to get you out of the way while she oversees Isaac's upbringing. What better way than to send you and Dommel off on an extended honeymoon?"

"Will you stop spouting moonshine?" Looking around, she motioned to a woman dressed in layers of diaphanous material. She asked the woman to give her one length of fabric. She bound it around Neville's shoulder.

"Mayhap I was premature sending for the doctor." His smile was a bit steadier. "You have a real skill, Pris."

"From the many times I have patched up Isaac's knees. That will hold for now, but I would prefer to have Dr. Dommel examine it." She glanced at where the men had been fighting.

One was lying on the ground, moaning. Mr. Birch, she noted, not surprised. He seemed to be about whenever knives were. A crowd was gathering, and she wondered if they thought this was for their entertainment. Relief bubbled through her when she saw a familiar face.

She called, "Vicar Kenyon, will you tend to that man while I make sure Neville waits quietly for the doctor?"

"Of course." The reverend's face was long with dismay, and his red mustache drooped. Pushing through the gawking crowd, he squatted and began speaking to Mr. Birch in a consoling voice.

Priscilla put her arm around Neville. Helping him to his feet, she said, "Easy."

"I am fine, Pris."

"Are you? You still look as if you are ready to swoon."

He tried to chuckle, but it came out in a groan.

He leaned on her as they walked to the house. Guests and performers moved aside to let them pass through the oddly silent throng. Guiding him into the house, she asked a footman to direct them to the nearest room.

Neville took only a pair of steps into the room before dropping to sit on a chair. It was, Priscilla noted, a room being used to hold supplies for the Faire. Bottles of wine were lined up on one table, and glasses and china arranged on others.

"Pour some wine for us, please," she said to the footman.

"But Lord Stenborough—"

"Will be dismayed if one of his guests is not attended to."

The footman did not argue. He opened a bottle and filled two glasses.

Priscilla took one and handed it to Neville. The other she set on the table beside the red-tufted chair where he sat. Thanking the footman, she sent him to let Dr. Dommel know they were waiting in this cluttered room.

"You should know better than to jump into the middle of a knife fight, Neville," she said as soon as the footman had left.

"I could not resist playing the hero for you."

"You need to recall this is not one of your stage productions."

Neville took another sip of wine, then gritted his teeth as a pulse of agony raced down his arm. When Priscilla leaned toward him, he wanted to pull her closer and let her sweet kisses soothe away the pain. Instead he motioned her away. She did not need blood staining her costume as well. That would upset her and the children more.

"Are you sure you are all right?" she asked.

"I am going to be fine."

"You look awful."

"Not as bad as you did when you keeled over." He chuckled, glad he could.

She did not answer as she held out the other glass.

He looked down at the empty one in his hand. He had not realized he had finished it. Mayhap it would dull the sharp burning in his shoulder. Instead of taking the glass, he leaned his head back against the chair.

Blast it! Priscilla was right. He had been a fool to try to stop the fight. There was enough trouble without him trying to find more. Priscilla had every right to chastise him for being an idiot. Not that he had much of a defense. He *had* been stupid.

"Pris, I am sorry that I knocked you senseless."

"It wasn't your fault. Try this."

He opened his eyes to see Priscilla's face close to his. His fingers were sifting through her hair, drawing her mouth to his, before a single thought formed in his mind. Or mayhap it was as simple as kissing her was his only thought now. He savored the dulcet warmth of her mouth before she reached up and moved his hand away.

"Try *this*," she said, her voice soft and inviting. She pressed some small cloths over the wound.

He set his hand over hers. "I like your kisses better, Pris."

"I like it better when you are not bleeding." She slid her fingers from beneath his, and he gripped the cloths. Going to the door, she peered out. "Where is that doctor? I thought Mr. Harmsworth would hurry."

He laughed tightly. "He is probably off in some dusky corner trying to figure out how to tell Stenborough about this, leaving you to worry about me. I am touched by your nursing, Pris."

She put her finger to his temple. "You are touched right here. Wait quietly while I find what is keeping Dr. Dommel."

"I will just sit here and bleed."

Her steps faltered, and she faced him. "Don't tease me now, Neville."

"You look as if you could use some hoaxing."

"It will not help when you are hurt and your friend is . . ."

He came to his feet, ignoring how his head spun. He understood what she could not say. She was fearful that Dommel was delayed because Duncan had taken a turn for the worse.

"What is this?" came a feminine voice from the doorway. "Oh, no! Is that blood?"

Priscilla rushed to keep Miss Young from coming in and collapsing in a swoon at Neville's feet. Calling an order over her shoulder for Neville to sit, she steered the young woman from the door and directly into Dr. Dommel's path.

The doctor started to frown, then offered a brilliant smile to Priscilla.

Pretending she had not seen it, she said, "Sir Neville is within. The gash in his shoulder is bleeding. Will you close it, Dr. Dommel?"

"A gash? The housekeeper could have sewn that for him." His nose wrinkled at the idea of doing such a menial task.

"Please, Dr. Dommel." She hated pretending she would welcome his attentions and wished he would remember his oath to tend to the sick and hurt. "I did not trust anyone but you to do this."

"I see." He chuckled. "As the wound is not serious—"

"Dr. Dommel, it is more than a simple scratch."

"Trust me to decide that, my lady."

Although she wanted to ask how he could make that determination without examining the patient, she said, "Of course." She did not want to delay him from going to Neville.

"I hope you will give me a similar answer when I ask if you would allow me to escort you to the birthday masquerade at the end of the Faire."

She stared at him, too shocked to speak. How could he be talking about this when Neville was *bleeding?*

"Your aunt assured me that you would be willing to let me escort you."

"Dr. Dommel—"

"Do offer your answer swiftly, if you will, my lady." He motioned toward the door. "My patient is waiting for you to decide."

She frowned. Was he saying that he would not tend to Neville if she rejected his invitation? Surely she must be hearing him wrong. She wondered what her aunt had said to the doctor to make him so eager for her company.

Not wishing to delay Neville's care any longer, she said, "Yes, Dr. Dommel, I will let you escort me to the masquerade. Now will you tend to Neville?"

"Certainly." He tweaked her cheek.

Priscilla scowled as he went into the room. Bother! First he coerced the answer he wanted to his invitation; then he treated her as if she were a child. She needed to hold her tongue while he tended to Neville.

When the door closed in her face, she started to open it. She paused when Miss Young asked, "Was that blood I saw on Sir Neville's coat and shirt?"

"He halted a fight among two members of the troupe, but he was hurt."

"That intolerable Mr. Birch was fighting, wasn't he?" she asked, startling Priscilla. "He is such a horrible man."

"Have you had a confrontation with Mr. Birch, too?"

She sat on a chair set in an alcove. "No, but I have heard tales." Her eyes widened. "One of you almost being impaled by his knife."

"'Twas an accident, and I was not injured." She did not want to discuss this with Miss Young. "Did Mr. Harmsworth tell you of it?"

"No. Lord Stenborough did." She giggled. "He was

lauding your bravery, my lady, which distressed Lady Stenborough greatly."

"Lady Priscilla, may I speak with you?" asked the man hurrying toward them.

"Mr. Bennett!" She smiled. Other than seeing Neville and Duncan hale, there was no one she had wanted to see more just now.

He bowed over her fingers. "I was told you were here."

"Have you met—?" She saw Miss Young walking away. How odd! Did Miss Young have a reason to avoid the manager of the troupe or had she another errand? She frowned. Miss Young had not explained why she had come here. Of all the people she had encountered at the Faire, Priscilla had considered Mr. Bennett the most normal. *Of course*, she added silently, *that does not mean much with this troupe*.

"How is Hathaway . . . um, Sir Neville?" asked Mr. Bennett.

"The doctor is taking care of him now."

"Doctor?" His face grew wan. "Is he badly hurt?"

"I believe he will be fine soon."

"Good, because I need him to tend to the men who were fighting." He released his breath slowly. "I had no idea such things awaited us here."

"Do not take this wrongly, Mr. Bennett, but may-hap now Lord Stenborough will see the wisdom of putting an end to this Faire."

"Moments ago he was adamant that nothing must curtail this celebration."

"So he would rather have his guests hurt one by one?"

Mr. Bennett shrugged. "That you need to ask him, my lady."

"Do you have these fights often?"

"We are one big, sometimes happy, family. Familiarity breeds—"

"Save me the clichés." She pointed toward the door. "Have you ever had someone hurt and murdered before?"

He rubbed his hands together. "One time. We had a tamed bear traveling with the show."

Priscilla's face grew cold. "Are you saying the bear attacked someone?"

"No!" He shuddered, hunching into himself. "If I may say so, my lady, you have a vivid imagination."

"So I have been told. What happened?"

"The bear trainer was a big Russian man named Sergei."

"Sergei what?"

"Just Sergei."

She glanced toward the door, wishing it would open so she could see how Neville fared. Trying to keep her attention on this conversation, she asked, "What happened to Sergei and his bear?"

"We think someone poisoned the bear. One morning it was dead. Sergei left." He sighed. "He drank a lot before the bear was found dead, and he drank more after."

"No one ever found out where he went?"

"Nobody would bother. Performers wander from one troupe to another in hope of better pay or to avoid trouble and their pasts."

The door opened, and Dr. Dommel peered out. The troupe's manager began to ask the doctor about Neville. Priscilla paid neither man any mind. She slipped past the doctor before he could halt her.

Neville was pacing between the tables. His shoulder was wrapped in bandages, creating a hump beneath the coat he still wore. Stubbornly wore, she suspected. She wanted to rush to him, but she could not forget that the doctor and Mr. Bennett were watching. She contented herself with asking Neville how he fared.

"He will be fine," Dr. Dommel said. "You need not fret on his behalf. If he takes care, he should be healed in a fortnight."

Priscilla glanced at Neville, who was opening and closing his left hand, testing it. He would take care only if he had no other choice.

"Thank you, Dr. Dommel," she said.

"You are welcome, my dear Lady Priscilla." He stepped in front of her, keeping her from going to Neville. "I trust I will see you at the activities this evening as well as before the masquerade."

"Is Mr. McAndrews well enough for you to leave his bedside that long?"

Dr. Dommel faltered, then said, "Mayhap on the morrow, then."

"Knowing Duncan is well would be the best tidings on the morrow."

"Yes. Yes . . . Yes, I see." The doctor picked up his bag and left with Mr. Bennett, who was trying to persuade him to help Mr. Birch.

Priscilla opened her mouth to ask Neville how he felt, but Mr. Harmsworth's voice intruded to ask, "Are you all right, Sir Neville?"

"I am fine." Neville's fingers brushed Priscilla's arm as he stepped past her. "Harmsworth, I had hoped to have a chance to speak with you. I have a few questions."

"I can assure you that I intend to speak to the troupe's manager immediately and express Lord Stenborough's wish that the two men who were fighting leave Stenborough Park before nightfall."

Neville waved aside the answer, then grimaced. When Priscilla refilled his glass of wine, he smiled his thanks before saying, "I had hoped to speak of another subject. The identity of the murderer."

"Are you asking if I have any idea who might have used the crossbow?"

"*Your* crossbow."

"Mine?" Mr. Harmsworth lowered himself to the chair. "I don't have a crossbow."

"You have one for your role as Robin Hood in the events to come."

"Yes, yes, but—"

"Priscilla found some purple feathers."

"Like the ones in Robin Hood's crossbow," he muttered. He jumped to his feet. "Sir Neville, if you are accusing me of—"

"Calm down," Priscilla said. "No one is accusing anyone of anything." She held out the second glass to him.

"I did take a lesson with it." Mr. Harmsworth took a deep drink. "Last night, before any guests arrived."

"Did anyone else take lessons?" Neville asked.

"Not when I did." He frowned. "The thing is blasted hard to load and shoot. I had help from several of the actors."

Neville glanced at her, but Priscilla had no idea what he was trying to convey with that intense look. Cradling his left elbow in his right hand, he asked, "Did any of the actors do or say anything that might have suggested antipathy toward the one playing the king?"

Mr. Harmsworth sat again. A strange expression crossed his face. "What makes you think Mr. McAndrews and Roland were the intended targets? That was a bustling, jostling crowd. They could have moved in front of someone at the wrong moment."

"Duncan was sitting."

"Then mayhap the archer was not such a good shot. Mayhap it was a lucky shot." He sighed. "Or an unlucky one. It could have been an accident. Look at what happened to Burr."

"It was not an accident at the banquet grounds!" Priscilla could keep quiet no longer. "Whether the quarrels found their intended targets or not, the fact is that someone fired that crossbow from a concealed spot and then returned it to its rack. Someone who must have hoped that suspicion would fall on someone else. In this case, you, Mr. Harmsworth. Do *you* have enemies among the troupe?"

He shook his head. "I never met them until yesterday. Lord Stenborough saw the troupe previously and asked me to arrange for them to play here. I had correspondence with Mr. Bennett, but that was the total of my knowledge of the troupe before they arrived." Pushing himself to his feet, he added, "I wish what happened today truly was an accident, but I know it was not." He finished the wine and put the glass on the table. Going to the door, he said, "Someone has a reason to kill. I hope we can find out why."

"We must," Priscilla replied. "If we fail, someone else could be hurt."

Neville added grimly, "You can wager your life on that."

NINE

"You are a hero, Uncle Neville!"

Priscilla halted Leah from throwing her arms around Neville. "A wounded hero."

Her daughter gave her a sheepish grin. "I will be careful."

"It is all right," Neville said, holding his right arm out to the young girl.

As he gave Leah a quick hug, Priscilla blinked back unexpected tears. She must never forget how important he was to her children. They had known him their entire lives, and they anticipated each of his visits with glee. If he had been injured more seriously . . . She shook that thought from her head.

She sat on a comfortable chair in the large room of the suite they had been offered by Lord Stenborough. As Isaac asked dozens of questions about the fight and each of Neville's answers became more outrageous than the one before, she saw her oldest coming on tiptoe toward her.

"Is Aunt Cordelia resting?" Priscilla asked when Daphne drew up a stool and sat beside her.

"Yes. The posset you sent worked beautifully."

"I sent?" Priscilla frowned. "I did not send a posset."

"But, Mama, the maid said—"

"Wait here." Coming to her feet, she hushed her daughter's questions. She heard Neville ask something, but waved an impatient hand at him.

Her aunt's room was filled with shadows because the draperies had been drawn, erasing any color from the carpet and the heavy furniture. Not waiting for her eyes to adjust to the murk, she hurried to the bed. Her foot hit a shoe, which bounced off an armoire. On the high bed, her aunt murmured something, but did not wake.

"You think she has been poisoned?" Neville whispered from behind her.

Priscilla was not astonished that he had ignored her request to stay in the other room. If their situations had been reversed, she would have been as unwilling to wait.

"I have no idea," she replied as quietly, picking up a glass from her aunt's bedside table. She took a sniff, then put it down and smiled. The scents of lettuce and oil of roses drifted from the glass. It was just what Daphne had said it was. A sleeping posset.

Motioning for Neville to lead the way from the bedchamber, Priscilla released the breath she had been holding. She closed the door and quickly assured the children nothing was amiss.

"I fear I am too jumpy," she said.

"You are wise to be concerned, Pris." He grimaced and put his hand to his shoulder. "Though, whoever sent that posset up here did you a great favor."

"And you." She smiled as she stroked his uninjured arm. "Aunt Cordelia would be making a May dance of you now."

"Mayhap the favor was to her." He chuckled. "With this vexing pain, I find it difficult to control my mouth."

"So you would speak your mind to her? That is no different from any other time."

"No, I was thinking rather of *not* controlling my mouth, like this."

She gasped as he pulled her up against him. Her protests that he was going to hurt his shoulder more vanished when his lips covered hers. She softened against him, wanting to find a sanctuary from the insanity, even though kissing him could lead to another very special sort of madness.

He raised his head, his teeth clenched. Not wanting to irritate him by reminding him that he was supposed to rest instead of engage in such delightful antics, she drew him to a chair.

He refused to sit.

Her exasperation focused on him. "Neville, you should rest."

"That is not easy here."

She looked at her children, who were gathered at the largest window, each one trying to talk more loudly than the others as they pointed out people they knew. "I understand. Do you want some help to get back to your tent?"

"Not now. I am going to find Dommel and get a report on Duncan's condition."

"I shall go with you so that when you fall on your face, I can remind you that you should be following the doctor's orders."

"Your compassion is vexing, Pris." Neville put his hands on Priscilla's shoulders. He had to fight their longing to stroke down her arms before circling her waist and bringing her up against his chest. "However, I would feel better if you remained here and kept a steady eye on your children."

"Why?"

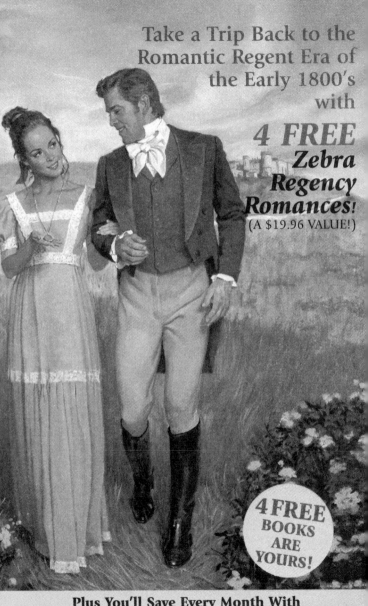

We'd Like to Invite You to Subscribe to Zebra's Regency Romance Book Club and Send You 4 Free Books as Your Introduction! (Worth $19.96!)

If you're a Regency lover, imagine the joy of getting 4 FREE Zebra Regency Romances and then the chance to have these lovely stories delivered to your home each month at the lowest price available! Well, that's our offer to you and here's how you benefit by becoming a Regency Romance subscriber:

- *4 FREE Introductory Regency Romances are delivered to your doorstep (you only pay for shipping & handling)*
- *4 BRAND NEW Regencies are then delivered each month (usually before they're available in bookstores)*
- *Subscribers save almost $4.00 off the cover price every month*
- *You also receive a FREE monthly newsletter, which features author profiles, discounts, subscriber benefits, book previews and more*
- *There's no risks or obligations…in other words, you can cancel whenever you wish with no questions asked*

Join the thousands of readers who enjoy the savings and convenience offered to Regency Romance subscribers. After your initial introductory shipment, you'll receive 4 brand-new Zebra Regency Romances each month to examine for 10 days. Then, if you decide to keep the books, you pay the preferred subscriber's price, plus shipping and handling.

It's a no-lose proposition, so return the FREE BOOK CERTIFICATE today!

4 FREE BOOKS are waiting for you! Just mail in the certificate below!

FREE BOOK CERTIFICATE

YES! Please rush me 4 FREE Zebra Regency Romances (I only pay $1.99 for shipping and handling).I understand that each month thereafter I will be able to preview 4 brand-new Regency Romances FREE for 10 days. Then, if I should decide to keep them, I will pay the money-saving preferred subscriber's price for all 4... (that's a savings of 20% off the retail price), plus shipping and handling. I may return any shipment within 10 days and owe nothing, and I may cancel this subscription at any time.

Name_____

Address_____Apt._____

City_____State_____Zip_____

Telephone (_____)_____

Signature_____

(If under 18, parent or guardian must sign)

Offer limited to one per household and not to current subscribers. Terms,
offer and prices subject to change. Orders subject to acceptance by
Regency Romance Book Club. Offer Valid in the U.S. only.   RN063A

Treat yourself to 4 FREE Regency Romances!
A $19.96 VALUE... FREE!
No obligation to buy anything ever!

lll..l..l.ll....lll.l.l..ll..l..lll..l..ll..lll..l

REGENCY ROMANCE BOOK CLUB
Zebra Home Subscription Service, Inc.
P.O. Box 5214
Clifton NJ 07015-5214

He wondered if any other woman would be so direct and calm when fear glowed in her eyes. If she had swooned as Lady Stenborough did at the merest mention of trouble, he would not have been able to depend on her as he did.

In a hushed voice so the children would not overhear, he replied, "Someone sent a posset for your aunt. It may have been with the best of intentions, but I think it would be for the best if one of us—you or me or your aunt—was with the children at all times until you take your leave."

"Bother! You are correct."

"Which quite obviously annoys you . . . almost as much as Dommel did when pressuring you to agree to have him escort you to the masquerade."

"You heard that?"

He put his hand over his heart, striking a pose that would have brought laughter from the children if they had been looking at him. "Pris, your sacrifice was far more than I would have asked of you."

"As I expect we shall be leaving Stenborough Park before then, it was no sacrifice."

"You are a devious woman." He smiled, although he had never felt less like doing so. The incision in his shoulder burned and ached at the same time, and he would have been delighted to sit here so Priscilla she could massage his temples and his mouth with kisses.

Before he could no longer resist that tempting image, Neville walked out. He heard, as he closed the door, Priscilla telling the children to have patience, but they must wait until their great-aunt woke before they returned to the Faire.

A few quick questions gained Neville directions to the room where Duncan was under Dr. Dommel's care. As he strode up the stairs and along the passage leading away from the Faire's noise, he prepared his arguments to force the doctor to realize it would be wise to allow Neville to see for himself how his friend fared. Mayhap Neville should remind him that ladies prefer to select their escorts, not to be forced in such a despicable manner. The pleasure of imagining how he would impress that upon the doctor kept him from thinking about how his head was beginning to throb in time with his shoulder.

Neville knocked, and the door opened.

Dr. Dommel peered out. "Sir Neville!"

"I want to see Mr. McAndrews. Now. I will brook with no discussion of why I should not see him."

"Discussion? I just sent a footman for you!" The doctor gave him a practiced smile. "I assume someone will send him back."

"Why did you send a footman?"

"Your friend is awake, and he wishes to speak with you."

Neville decided to accept victory. He paused on his way into the chamber, which was decorated in shades of blue and green that were almost black in the dim light, when he heard the doctor speak again.

"I will go and assure Lady Priscilla that her friend is doing better." Dommel needed only to add a cackling laugh to sound like a stage villain.

Blast! His smile returned when he saw a bell near a door that must lead into the bedroom. As soon as Dommel closed the door, Neville rang the small brass bell. He gave quick orders to the maid who answered his summons. She was to hurry to Lady Priscilla and interrupt Dr. Dommel's call. Only when she curtsied and hurried away did Neville release the breath he had been holding.

Poor Priscilla! She had her aunt admonishing her at every turn, and now she had an overly amorous doctor looking for any excuse to give her a look-in.

Neville chuckled. He would have enjoyed seeing Priscilla putting the doctor in his place, but that pleasure was not to be his. Instead he must speak with Duncan.

The room beyond the outer chamber also was swathed in shadows. He ignored the fancy furnishings as he walked to the bed that was more befitting a maharajah's palace than a country home. It appeared Stenborough's interest in inaccurate history did not focus totally on the medieval era.

"It is about time you got here," came a grumble from the bed.

Neville smiled. Duncan was propped against pillows mounded up against the fancily carved headboard where tigers and elephants were in some sort of battle.

Pulling a chair closer to the bed, he sat, not wanting his friend to guess he had been wounded, too. "Dr. Dommel seems to believe you have plenty of years ahead of you."

"Long enough to bounce your grandchildren on my knee."

"That may be a very long time, indeed."

"Don't hoax me. I saw how you were looking at the fair Priscilla. It confirms the gossip I have heard about the pair of you."

Although Neville had a peculiar curiosity about what was being said, most peculiar because he usually disdained such talk, he asked, "Did Dr. Dommel tell you what happened?"

"Don't you think I know when I have been shot?" Duncan pointed toward a table on the far side of the bed.

When Neville saw two pieces of a quarrel, he shook his head. "I did not think even *you* would be so grotesque as to save the weapon that almost killed you."

"Why not? How do you think this will look mounted and hanging over my mantel?"

"Better than having you stuffed and mounted there."

"Now who is grotesque?" Duncan started to chuckle, then grimaced as he pressed his hand to his side.

"Did you see anyone?"

His smile evaporated. "I saw many people. I was looking for you and Lady Priscilla. I saved seats for you near the king's chair. The man playing the king—which one was it?"

"Henry."

"No number?"

"Not anymore."

Duncan nodded. "I was afraid of that. I saw him hit, too."

"Did you see anything by the shrubs?" Neville was glad Priscilla was not here. She would be scolding him for asking Duncan these questions, but if Duncan could help them, they might be able to find the murderer before sunset.

For a long minute, Duncan did not answer. Neville did not hurry him. Duncan McAndrews had a mind for particulars and a nose for everyone's business. If anyone had seen anything and could recall it, it would be Duncan.

"There were several people by the bushes," Duncan said, staring across the room as if he could re-create the scene. "One was Garvin Harmsworth. He was talking with two women." His forehead wrinkled more deeply. "A blonde and a brunette. No, not blonde. Light brown, but she was a real looker."

"How about the other woman?" Neville did not bother to hide his annoyance. Duncan was no morose Scotsman. He admired women, and he liked to go on for hours about their charms. If Duncan changed the subject to women, the conversation might never get back to the interrupted banquet.

"I could not see too much of her, but she was a damned well constructed woman."

"Was she in costume?"

"In a short tunic and stockings."

Neville stared at his friend. "A short tunic? Are you sure it was a woman?"

"*It* was definitely a she. I may be getting older, but when it comes to women, my eyes are getting better."

"Your eyesight or your imagination?"

"I know what I saw. She had dark hair and lovely legs. I thought that might be my last sight, and it was an appealing one."

Neville walked around the bed. Staring at the quarrel, he wondered why he had not considered that Garvin Harmsworth might be behind this. He did not get along well with the actors, and he certainly, as Lord Stenborough's estate manager, would have access to the troupe's props. However, Duncan believed Harmsworth was innocent, and Neville trusted his friend's instincts.

He glanced at Duncan. His friend was very pale, so leaving might be a good idea. He could come back later. Mayhap, after a few hours of peace and quiet, he would have more questions and Duncan would have more answers.

"Rest, my friend," he said as he went toward the door.

"Are you leaving to rescue fair Priscilla from the good doctor?"

"You don't need to look for drama everywhere, Duncan."

"I don't have to. It seems to find me." He shifted and winced. "Dr. Dommel was talking endlessly about how my dear friend Priscilla would be so happy to hear of my recovery. Did I miss something while I was unconscious? Have you let the lady slip through your hands and into the doctor's?"

"Leave off, Duncan."

"I thought *you* might be taking Priscilla and the children back to the Faire, instead of allowing Dr. Dommel to call on her."

"I have no idea what Priscilla has planned." He did not like deceiving his friend, but he had no interest in talking about Dr. Dommel's devious attempts to woo Priscilla.

"Surely you have given thought to the fact that the children will give you an excellent alibi to figure out why this happened. Youngsters like to poke their noses into many different places and ask outrageous questions that could lead you to the truth."

His laugh sounded forced. *Probably because it was*, he thought. "Constable Forshaw is handling the investigation."

"The constable?"

"The local man from Stonehall-on-Sea."

"The one who believed fair Priscilla was a murderess?"

Neville regretted telling that story to his friend on

the way down from London. "Yes. He is a good man."

"A good man is not what is needed now. A man with a touch of the devil about him is needed to chase down the person who used that crossbow." He sighed, and his face revealed his pain. Every line in his face was dug in as if with a potter's strong hand. "You must find this archer, Neville. I know you know how to get to the bottom of anything. This should be as easy as A-B-C for you."

"Easy? Duncan, while you have been asleep, we have been looking everywhere we can think of."

"We? You and Lady Priscilla?"

"Yes."

His smile returned, weak. "Good." Then he sighed again. "Not that you will find anything now that the Faire has come to an end."

"It is still going on."

"Still?" Duncan's mouth worked, but no more sounds came out.

"Are you all right?" Neville hoped his friend was not suffering some sort of seizure.

He wheezed, "Even the tournament?"

"Tournament?" A sick cramp in his stomach matched the desperation in his friend's voice.

"Stenborough was telling me about it this morning." He leaned forward, pain scoring his face. "Neville, you have to stop that tournament. Stop it before someone else gets killed."

TEN

Neville hated when Duncan was right. Usually his
friend argued on and on. Then, wearing one of his
superior grins, he would laugh, and Neville would
know Duncan had been debating solely for the en-
joyment of it. But Duncan *was* right today. That
blasted tournament had to be stopped before there
was more trouble. What was Stenborough thinking?
The answer to that was simple. Stenborough was not
thinking of anything but celebrating his dashed
birthday.

When his knock on Priscilla's door was answered
by June, he did not wait for the maid's complete explanation that Lady Priscilla, her aunt, and the
children had left a short while ago. He strode away
at a pace that caused his headache to worsen. He
paid it no more mind than he did anyone he passed.
Priscilla should have waited for him to return before
she went to the Faire with the children. It was dangerous. Her curiosity could lead her to disaster.

He went out of the house and crossed the open
field toward the Faire. The gaiety had not lessened.
In fact, the many bottles emptied of wine had added
to the frivolity. He edged through the press of people, taking care to protect his arm. Seeing several

people point at him, he guessed they believed his bloody coat was part of the Faire.

Fools!

Where had all these people come from? Half the shire must have joined the invited guests. Neville scanned the grounds, glad he could see over most heads. Forshaw was not in sight. Too bad. He would have liked to have the constable with him when he found Stenborough.

Trumpets blared. Flat, he noted, as he came around the back of the castle. He stared at the field that was now set for a joust. A shoulder-high wooden wall ran along the center. At either end stood a small striped tent with a brightly colored banner fluttering in the warm breeze. Red on one tent, purple on the other. Horses were being walked in circles to keep them from reacting to the noise from the crowd hemming the field. A pavilion draped with red, purple, and green bunting was waiting for Stenborough, his lady, and their exulted guests.

"It is a surprisingly accurate jousting field, isn't it?"

Neville heard dismay in Priscilla's voice. That she had been able to come this close without him taking note warned him how dulled his senses were. Like him, she had dispensed with her costume. He would have enjoyed admiring her light blue gown . . . if the throbbing along his blasted skull were not causing his eyes to blur. "The jousting area is accurate and potentially deadly."

When she put one hand on his arm, he started to smile. That expression became a frown when she pressed the back of her other hand against his forehead.

"Leave off, Pris."

"You are too warm. You should be resting."

"Have you given thought to the idea *you* are the reason I am so warm?"

Priscilla frowned. Even Neville's voice was not as strong as it should be, and his every motion was as stiff as an old man's. She knew it was worthless to reason with him. He would not rest until he identified the archer.

"How does Duncan fare?" she asked. Mayhap speaking of his friend would remind him of the dangers of overdoing things.

"Awake and sore and cross as crabs." He looked past her. "Pris, where is Stenborough?"

"Are you going to try to convince him to halt this tournament?"

The horns blared again.

"Yes. Have you seen him or Forshaw?"

She shook her head. "I have been looking for the constable. He must be on the grounds somewhere."

"Where are the children and your aunt?" he asked, his gaze coming back to her.

"They are fine. Leah and Isaac are having a conversation with one of the young actors. Daphne is watching over them, as are Dr. Dommel and my aunt."

"Who are probably discussing your wedding."

"Don't be absurd." She dimpled. "They will be discussing the betrothal party first."

"How did you slip away?"

She laughed. "If I tell you, I would never be able to use the same trick with you, Neville."

"Do you want to slip away from me?" His hand cupped her chin.

"Neville, this is not the time . . ." She closed her eyes, savoring the tingles flowing outward from where his thumb brushed her cheek.

"When will be?" he whispered, bending toward her.

Before she could answer, he swayed and cursed. She grasped his uninjured arm to keep him from toppling off his feet. "When you can be sensible!"

"That will be a very long time, I fear. I may have no more sense than our host."

As if on cue, Lord Stenborough came barreling toward them. Priscilla grimaced when she saw that he wore a doublet and stockings even more garish than the previous ones. Green stockings made his legs look like two overripe squash.

"Hathaway! Are you all right?" he asked, nearly running Priscilla down. As she edged out of the way, a flush climbed his bulbous cheeks. "Forgive me, Lady Priscilla. I did not see you there. It has been a long and busy day."

"Then have a quiet evening," she replied.

"Quiet? Nonsense! We are going to have a tournament. It will be the *pièce de résistance* for the day, just as the ball shall be tomorrow evening."

"Holding a tournament when a murderer may be nearby is insane."

"Murderer? I thought we agreed that unfortunate incident was an accident."

She gave him what she hoped was a withering glare. "You must stop this."

Lord Stenborough motioned toward the field. "If it would make you feel better, you can inspect the place yourself."

"Thank you," Neville said, his voice as rigid as his mouth. "We will."

"If you see Harmsworth around, tell him we are ready to begin."

"We will." Taking her arm, he added, "Come along, Pris."

She waited until their voices would not reach back to Lord Stenborough before saying, "You do not need to drag me about."

"I did not want Stenborough to have a chance to change his mind."

"Why should he? He has convinced himself that everything that has happened has been *accidental.*"

"You don't need to make it sound like an obscenity."

"It is," she insisted, "when someone else could get hurt."

Priscilla said nothing more as she went with him toward the purple tent.

He opened the tent flap, peered in, then pulled it aside. "Go ahead, Pris." His voice shook on each word.

"Are you sure you can—?"

"I am fine!"

Beads of sweat lathered his hair to his forehead and she wanted to retort that he was far from fine. A greeting came from the tent, giving her no chance to do so.

"Come in, my lady."

Priscilla bent past the open flap and saw Garvin Harmsworth dressed in what looked like a quilted waistcoat and breeches. No wonder Neville's voice had been uneven. He had been trying not to laugh at Mr. Harmsworth's ensemble.

When perspiration cascaded along Mr. Harmsworth's face, she wondered why he was wearing such heavy clothes. He reached for a silvery item hanging on a mannequin, and she realized it was part of a suit of armor.

"You heard him. Enter, my lady," ordered Neville.

When she glowered at him, he chuckled. She was surprised Mr. Harmsworth did not laugh while he stepped aside to make room for them in the cramped tent. A dozen questions bounced through her head as tension laced the air, constricting each breath.

"Lady Priscilla," said Mr. Harmsworth, as he ran his hand nervously over the metal vest he had put on. "It is kind of you to take time to come and see me before this match."

"I would rather talk you out of participating."

He shook his head. "Lord Stenborough is insistent that someone represent Stenborough Park at the lists, and I was given the honor of doing so."

"The unfortunate honor."

"I am pleased to be able to serve Lord Stenborough in this manner." He raised his chin as pride slipped into his words. "I am the best rider among his lordship's men."

"But you cannot have much experience at the lists."

"I have been practicing."

"With jousts as well as with crossbows?"

"Yes." Without a pause to let her ask another question, he asked, "Sir Neville, how are you?"

"Not as good as I would like to be, but not as bad as I have been at other times." A smile quirked at the corner of his mouth.

"Have you seen Mr. McAndrews? How is he faring?"

"He is awake."

Mr. Harmsworth brightened. "That is good to hear."

"And he is remembering things that might help us find the person who fired the quarrels."

"Things?" Priscilla asked. "What things?"

Neville started to shrug, then put his hand up to his wounded shoulder. She wanted to tell him that his nonchalant posture was wasted on her because she knew how distressed he was.

"Duncan mentioned people he saw and sounds he heard just before he was wounded," he said.

"Who specifically?" asked Mr. Harmsworth.

"I will make you a deal," he said with a taut smile. "If you get Stenborough to put a stop to the tournament, I will tell you what Duncan told me."

"That is ridiculous!" Mr. Harmsworth's fingers tightened around the pole in the middle of the tent. "And blackmail."

"Blackmail?" Priscilla asked, astonished. "Why would you say that?"

Mr. Harmsworth looked everywhere but at Priscilla. "I fear I spoke foolishly."

"He is concerned," Neville said quietly, "that Duncan mentioned seeing him near the bush where you found the feather. Don't worry, Harmsworth. He mentioned only that he saw you speaking with a pair of women."

"Yes, yes, I was." Mr. Harmsworth wore a sheepish grin. "Two of the maids who were supposed to serve the meal that was never served."

"From Stenborough Park?"

"Yes."

"Why was one dressed as a man?"

Priscilla frowned. "One was in male clothing?"

"It was Lord Stenborough's wish," Mr. Harmsworth replied quickly, "that there be an equal number of male and female servers at the banquet. As we have a few more maids than footmen, that seemed an obvious solution."

"An unusual one, I would say." She rubbed her hand against her nape, wishing she had put up her hair before she came into this hot tent. "As unusual as those quilted garments you are wearing, Mr. Harmsworth."

"I wear this to protect myself from the armor." He pointed at the pieces still draped over the figure. "Lord Stenborough had a suit of armor designed for me. I would be ungrateful to leave it sitting on the dobble."

She realized he was referring to the mannequin. "It must have cost him dearly."

"More than three-hundred-fifty pounds."

Neville opened the door flap. "Come on, Pris. Harmsworth does not need you interrogating him before he rides."

She frowned at him. *He* had been the one asking questions. "Is the armor made of iron?"

"Yes." Mr. Harmsworth handed her a piece to examine. "I was surprised how light it was. The whole of it, with the undergarments, weighs less than six stone. So I can become a dashing knight in shining armor to defend Stenborough Park's honor." He picked up a helmet topped with a purple plume. "If that is still possible."

Priscilla glanced at Neville, then back at Mr. Harmsworth. "Is something else amiss?"

"I do not know." Mr. Harmsworth sat and buckled his metal shin guards in place. "Mayhap the day's events are settling in."

"Then persuade Stenborough to rethink this," Neville said.

Keeping his head down, he said, "I have mentioned it to him, but he will not heed me. He keeps saying nothing else will happen."

"You cannot be sure of that."

"I can be certain Lord Stenborough will not change his mind. He has been planning this celebration for a long time. Yet I cannot shake off this feeling he is wrong."

"We agree with you, Mr. Harmsworth." Priscilla put her hand out to keep him from reaching for the next piece of armor. "I think there is something else brewing out there."

"Get me proof, and I will take it to Constable Forshaw myself."

Dampening her abruptly dry lips, she said, "I do not have any proof, but you might."

"Me?"

She took the helmet from Neville. The slit to see through was so narrow she wondered if Mr. Harmsworth would be blind when he wore it. Running her finger along the purple plume, she asked, "Do you know how many other props have purple feathers?"

Mr. Harmsworth's face went white, then red, then gray, all in the course of a single breath. He shook his head. "I do not know how many, but—" He looked up at her. "I can tell you that I did not fire those quarrels."

"Duncan confirmed that." Her eyes widened. "Neville, if we ask Lord Stenborough to postpone the tournament because Duncan asked . . ."

"He will not listen." Mr. Harmsworth sighed. "And mayhap he is right. If we pretend everything is as it should be, mayhap we can lure the murderer out into the open again."

"Who is going to volunteer to be the bait?"

He stood and reached for the next piece of armor. "All we can do is keep our eyes open and be ready to react."

"To what?"

"To anything," said Neville with a sigh. He pushed the flap aside. "Harmsworth, will you join me and Lady Priscilla for supper after the tournament? If we work together to seek a solution, we might be able to find this murderer."

A smile creased his face. "That sounds like an excellent plan." He hesitated, then cleared his throat. "Lord Stenborough . . ."

"I believe we can leave Stenborough to his revels," Neville replied, earning another grateful smile from Mr. Harmsworth.

Priscilla stepped out of the tent. She watched Neville closely while they walked to where the guests had gathered for the tournament. In the light from the setting sun, his coloring appeared better than earlier. His steps were steadier. Although she knew that such a wound would not slow him long, she hoped he was not pretending to be more hale than he was. She had never seen him on the stage, where he had been on his way to acclaim before he inherited his title, but she had witnessed him playing many roles since.

"Where are we going?" She frowned when she saw her children standing alone. Where was her aunt? "Bother!"

"Bother what?"

Instead of answering, Priscilla motioned to her children. They seemed to notice her at the same time and pushed through the crowd. She was glad to see that Daphne held hands with her sister and brother.

"Mama!" cried Isaac, running to her. "You need to come and see the snakes they have in a cage."

"Mama!" added Leah, close on his heels. "Jaspar said I could help him gather up the props after the tournament."

"Mama," said Daphne as she rolled her eyes, "they have been prattling nonstop since you left us. My ears are ringing as if I stood inside the bell at St. Elizabeth's."

Putting her arm around her oldest, Priscilla calmed her younger children by shuddering at Isaac's description of the snakes and by smiling when Leah spoke about the lad she had met. She was not afraid of snakes, but Isaac liked to think she was weakhearted so he could protect her. Leah accepted—however reluctantly—that her mother must meet this young man before giving permission to help.

"You are considering letting her help?" murmured Neville as they led the children toward the pavilion where the guests were finding seats.

"Not unless you or I or Aunt Cordelia is watching over her."

"Speaking of your dear aunt, I believe she is trying to get your attention."

Priscilla saw her aunt waving at her from the pavilion. Beside her, Dr. Dommel sat next to an empty seat. Dismay swirled through her. She appreciated that the doctor had come to let her know how Duncan fared, but her hints that she did not want his attentions, even though she had acceded to his demands about the masquerade, had not altered his knowing smiles. Although she had been tempted to ask him exactly what he thought he knew, she had curbed her tongue.

"We could watch the tournament from here," Neville said, warning that she was letting her reaction show.

Isaac ran toward the pavilion, shouting for them to hurry or they would miss the beginning of the tournament.

With a wry grin, Priscilla said, "You spoke a moment too late, Neville. To own the truth, I would be much happier if you were sitting somewhere out of the sunshine."

"Do not hover around me." He drew her hand into his arm while they went after the children. "I have always appreciated that you do not constantly try to tell me what to do."

"As you do me?"

"That is different. It is a gentleman's duty to watch over a lady."

Her reply was halted because they had reached the pavilion. They squeezed past other guests, heading toward her aunt. The space between the seats would have been a comfortable width, save for the full-skirted costumes so many women wore. She was glad she had changed.

"Go ahead," Neville said in a near whisper as he lowered his arm from beneath her hand.

"Where are you going?"

"I should have guessed I could not take my leave for even a moment without you questioning me." He pointed toward her aunt, greeting the children. "You shall have a front-row seat in case something happens."

"Where will you be?"

"Making sure nothing happens," he replied grimly.

Looking across the field, she put her hand on his uninjured arm. "I am uneasy about this."

"So am I."

Her hand constricted, crushing his sleeve. "You are? Then why are you acting as if you do not have a care?"

"I will meet you after the tournament."

Priscilla watched him slip out of the pavilion. She

realized that he must want to check something while everyone else was busy with the tournament. What had he taken note of that she had missed?

Edging around the other guests, she vowed that she would ask him to explain when they had a late meal with Mr. Harmsworth. A smile eased her tight lips when she saw several vacant chairs behind her aunt and on the opposite side of where Dr. Dommel sat. She slipped along that row.

Leaning over the chair in front of her, she greeted her aunt with a kiss before sitting in one of the empty chairs. Her aunt turned to frown, but Dr. Dommel sat down when two more guests came along the row. Miss Young was walking in front of a man Priscilla did not know.

"Lady Priscilla!" Miss Young chirped. Dropping to sit beside Priscilla, she smoothed her elegant bright blue gown around her. The medieval costume flattered her full curves. "I am pleased I could sit with you." She smiled at the man behind her. "Lady Priscilla, have you met Lord Byron?"

"The writer?" asked Priscilla as the man, who was dressed in a somber black that suggested he was in mourning, bowed over her hand.

He straightened, his curly hair bouncing about his head. He was an uncommonly handsome man with fine, regular features and a cleft in his chin. The smile on his full lips glowed in his eyes as he said, "I am honored that you know of my work."

"My late husband greatly admired your *English Bards and Scotch Reviewers*. He found the satire very amusing."

"May I?" He gestured to an empty chair beside her.

"Of course." As he sat, she asked, "Have you had anything else published, Lord Byron?"

"I hope to have more poetry published soon. I worked on a poem during my travels on the Continent that I believe may be worthy of publication."

"I did not realize you wrote poetry as well as satire."

"I aspire to write poetry that will capture the hearts of all who read it."

Miss Young laughed. "I cannot imagine anything you wrote not being deeply touching, my lord."

Priscilla listened, amused, as the young woman flirted with the handsome baron. When Lord Byron stood, excusing himself so he might greet a friend, Miss Young sighed.

"What a somber fellow," Miss Young said as soon as Lord Byron could no longer hear them.

"He seems quite serious about his work."

"I believe he is. Edwin—Lord Stenborough mentioned that." Color flashed up her face, and Priscilla knew Miss Young had not intended to use their host's given name. "Lord Stenborough also mentioned that Lord Byron's mother recently died."

Priscilla looked at where the baron was talking with another woman who was gushing something to him. "I wish I had known to offer my condolences."

"I was told not to mention it because Lord Byron does not wish to speak of it." Miss Young grinned. "I do believe the tournament is about to begin. I hope you can enjoy it."

"I will try."

"I know how upset you *must* be," she said. "First Sir Neville's friend is hurt, then he is, as well."

"I trust no one else shall be. If—" She gasped when a sharp object jabbed between her and Miss Young.

Her eyes followed what she realized was a lance,

and she looked up to see a white horse, atop of which sat a knight in armor covered by a bright purple surcoat. He flipped back his visor and she saw Mr. Harmsworth's cheery grin.

"Lady fair," he murmured as he bowed toward her.

Hearing the whispers among the spectators, Priscilla grimaced.

He laughed as he pulled off a mail glove and rubbed the back of his neck. "Lady Priscilla, do not look angry. I thought you would like to be my lady fair for this joust."

Miss Young muttered something under her breath, and Aunt Cordelia turned to fire a fearsome frown in Priscilla's direction. Beside her, Isaac was jumping to his feet and cheering while Leah and Daphne seemed to be sharing a fit of giggles.

"Did Neville ask you to do this?" Priscilla asked, wondering if Neville had gone back to speak with Mr. Harmsworth.

"Lord Stenborough did. He thought you would like to have a part in the tournament. He thought it might ease your mind about . . ." His grin faded.

"Find someone else, please."

He nodded and drew back the lance. She expected him to turn to Miss Young and was astonished when he bowed toward her aunt and asked, "My lady, would you be willing to let me be your champion?"

Priscilla was shocked when her aunt agreed. Then she smiled. After all, her aunt had charmed three men into marrying her, and had caught Mr. McAndrews's attention. It should be no surprise that Mr. Harmsworth was paying her this honor. When the estate manager gave her a kerchief to tie around his wrist, she wondered if this had been his intention all along. His smile was warm when he bowed his head to Aunt Cordelia. Mayhap Miss Young was not the only one enjoying the chance for a bit of dallying amid the festivities. Mayhap it was her aunt's way of trying to forget the appalling events.

Priscilla sighed, wishing *she* could forget. Scanning the field, she saw another rider on the opposite side of the meadow. Laughter drifted to her, and she guessed the actor in the red surcoat had lured a woman into agreeing to portray his lady fair.

"Isn't this *so* exciting?" Miss Young asked, her smile returning. "You are too shy, Lady Priscilla. *I* would have been delighted to have someone riding for my honor."

"You are greatly enjoying the Faire."

"Oh, yes! Being stuck in the country is so boring, except for now at this Faire. I would love to go to Town, but I have never had the opportunity until lately."

"How did you find being in Town?"

"I have not gone yet, but I shall soon." She folded her hands in her lap as a satisfied smile wafted across her lips. "I suspect we shall go shortly after the Faire is over."

Priscilla knew better than to ask whom Miss Young intended to travel with. Clearly Miss Young had found someone eager to introduce her to London—a gentleman who was willing to have this pretty miss at his side.

As the two knights rode to opposite ends of the field, a raspy voice said from behind her, "I believe you are sitting in my seat."

Priscilla smiled at Lady Stenborough. "Excuse me. Of course, you can have it."

"Not you. Her." She pointed at Miss Young. *"My*

husband arranged for me to sit here." She smiled at
Priscilla. "Dear Edwin always thinks of me first and
foremost. He is such a doting husband."

Miss Young scowled, but rose, moving toward the
far end of the row. When she looked back, Priscilla
was astonished to see tears on her face. Lady Stenborough had been rude, that was true, but that did
not explain why Miss Young was weeping.

Lady Stenborough lowered her full form onto the
chair next to Priscilla. Folding her hands on the lap
of her ornate gown, she gazed at the field where the
evening heat shimmered above the grass. The thick
odor of her perfume threatened to choke Priscilla.

"I have been looking forward to this." She tilted
her chin as she added, "Having a tournament was
my idea, you know. After all, what is a Faire without
a tournament?"

"I had no idea that you were involved in planning
the Faire."

"Why shouldn't *I* be involved in arranging my
husband's birthday celebration?" Her full bosom
rose as she took a deep breath. "*I* am his wife, not
his . . ." She glared in the direction of Miss Young.

Priscilla understood what she should have when
she saw Miss Young's tears. Miss Young must be Lord
Stenborough's mistress, as Neville had guessed. That
he had invited her to his wife's house showed a
streak of cruelty Priscilla had not guessed he had. No
wonder Miss Young had left as soon as Lady Stenborough ordered her to do so. If anyone cared to
hear Priscilla's opinion, she would have found it difficult not to state that the viscount and his wife
deserved each other because neither of them
seemed to care about anyone else.

"And," Lady Stenborough continued in a voice

that reached to each corner of the covered pavilion, "I should have a say in this Faire because it is being funded by the dower money received from my father when Edwin and I were married."

"Your dower money?"

"You know how such things are. Sometimes there is money to spare and at other times, the upkeep of the estate drains away so much."

Priscilla did understand. She remembered Neville's comments about Lord Stenborough's gambling losses. That left the couple doomed to continue in this loveless marriage—or a marriage that was loveless on the viscount's side, for he made no secret of his admiration for every woman he met. She had seen him ogle Orysia and one of the other actresses in addition to Miss Young and herself. Lady Stenborough must have seen it as well, but a bill of divorce would be not only humiliating but very expensive, if it were possible at all. The viscount's adultery would not provide sufficient cause.

"Mayhap it would have been better," she said, "if you had arranged a different birthday celebration for your husband."

"Edwin wanted something special. Once he heard this troupe was available, he would have nothing else." Lady Stenborough sighed deeply. "I warned him that I had heard they had caused trouble elsewhere. Now it seems that one caused so much trouble someone followed the troupe here and murdered the poor man."

"Is that what you believe happened?" Priscilla wondered why she had not discussed this idea with Neville. The answer was simple. She had not imagined the dead actor had made an enemy who had come seeking revenge. It was a comforting idea until she recalled someone saying the man had no enemies.

A trumpet squealed for attention. She appraised both horses and riders. Nothing seemed amiss. Mayhap she was worrying needlessly. She wondered where Neville was. She would feel less anxious if he returned to tell her that he had found nothing wrong.

Another trumpet blast sent a wave of whispered anticipation through the pavilion. She gripped the chair in front of her as both riders raised their lances. In the middle of the field, a young man held up a flag. He shouted and dropped it. As hoofbeats pounded, he leaped back.

And, she saw with a burst of horror, someone leaped forward directly into the path of the horses.

ELEVEN

Near Bennett's wagon, Neville heard screams replace the cheers at the tournament grounds.

"What is it now?" asked the troupe's manager.

Neville did not answer. He rushed toward the tournament field, paying no attention to how his shoulder burned as he swung his arm. He recognized the sound of voices rising in horror. What was happening?

His breath caught, even more painful than the wound in his shoulder, when he saw Priscilla running across the grass in a path that would cross the horses'. What was she doing? She did not usually act so out of hand. More shrieks erupted. Among other cries, he heard Priscilla's children calling to her. More shrill than any of it, a horse whinnied at an impossibly high pitch.

He shouted her name and ran toward her. He would not reach her in time. Then he saw another form in the very middle of the field. Another woman!

As he raced closer, Priscilla hunched her shoulders and struck the other woman, sending her crashing to the ground, out of the way of the horses. Then she spun. Harmsworth's horse was racing toward her at top speed, the jousting lance pointed at her.

Neville threw himself forward, grasping her at the waist. They hit the wooden wall, and every ounce of breath was pummeled out of him. He collapsed atop her as the horse raced by.

Soft material brushed his face, and he heard, "Are you out of your mind?"

"Me? What about you? *You* ran in front of a horse." He looked down at Priscilla.

With her hair tousled around her shoulders, there was a softness about her she so seldom showed to anyone but her children. He was not sure if he wanted to scold her for being foolish or to kiss her because . . . He did not need a reason to want to kiss her. His fingers burrowed into her hair as his lips claimed hers.

He savored the rapid pulse of her breath, which grew even more swift as he deepened the kiss, wanting to imprint its flavor within his mouth. Even when he heard anxious voices, he did not raise his head. The very idea of her being hurt or killed had shaken him to depths he had not guessed existed.

A moan as Neville shifted his shoulder shattered the moment's pleasure. His moan of pain. Priscilla helped him sit.

"Are you all right?" he asked.

"I am fine. What about you?" Priscilla looked away from his eyes, which snapped with fury and the more powerful emotion she had discovered on his lips, to the lance that was driven into the wall only a few feet away.

He gripped his bandaged shoulder. "Of all the want-witted, bacon-brained, pudding-headed—"

"You have made yourself clear," she mumbled, tasting blood. She must have cut her lip, but she had not noticed its sting until now.

"You could have been killed!"

"So could have Miss Young."

"Miss Young?"

Priscilla pushed herself to her feet and, paying no attention to the crowd encircling them, went to where Miss Young lay like a cast-off doll. Kneeling, she brushed strands of red hair back from Miss Young's face.

"Someone bring some cool water!" she called. "Or *sal volatile.*"

Neville wove toward them, squatting to put his arms beneath the senseless woman.

"Leave her be," Priscilla said. "Let someone else carry her from the field before you injure your shoulder worse."

He drew his hands back. "Blast it, Pris! You know how to ruin a man's fantasy of seeing himself as a hero."

She smiled as short arms were flung around her. After hugging her son, she sat him on the grass beside her and smiled up at her daughters. She assured them she was fine, and was glad to hear that with some help from her friends her aunt was recovering in their tent from her dismay about her niece's ill-advised attempts to protect Miss Young.

Neville raised Miss Young's head and tapped her cheek. Her lush lashes fluttered, and her eyes opened. For a moment, confusion was in them; then a coy smile tipped her lips.

"Oh, Sir Neville, you rescued me!"

"From your own folly," Priscilla answered, not bothering to correct the young woman. "Why were you walking across the field just as the joust was beginning?"

"I was—" Two luminous tears dropped along her face. "My mind was wandering."

"So you followed it?" Neville shook his head. "You must take more care, Miss Young."

She pressed her fingers to her bodice. "I would be so pleased if you would call me Jessamyn. After all, you saved my life, Sir Neville."

"You are in error."

She grasped his hand between hers. "I am ever so grateful to you. I have never had a gentleman risk all for me, and I owe you a great duty, Sir Neville."

Whether Neville corrected Miss Young or not, Priscilla did not hear because Dr. Dommel asked, "Are you hurt, my lady?"

All these flirtatious games, which seemed to cajole otherwise competent minds to ignore everything else around them, were becoming tiresome. She let her frustration slip into her voice as she said, "Dr. Dommel, it would behoove you to check Miss Young first, for she may be hurt far worse than anyone else."

"But, my lady! I saw how Sir Neville knocked you aside. You must be bruised." His gaze swept along her body, and she knew he would be glad to examine every inch of her flesh.

"Dr. Dommel, your concerns are commendable, but please turn your attention to Miss Young. I cannot bear the thought of her suffering a moment longer."

She heard a muffled laugh. At first, she thought it came from Neville; then she saw her oldest child covering her mouth with her hand. Daphne's eyes twinkled mischievously.

Dr. Dommel motioned for them to move aside so he might examine Miss Young. The prone woman released Neville's hand, doing so only when he promised to call later to see how she fared.

Priscilla was grateful for Neville's help in coming to her feet, although she saw the acrimonious glare Miss Young fired at her when he did so. It was as cold as the expression she had worn when banished from her seat by Lady Stenborough. Had Miss Young turned her affections so swiftly from the viscount to Neville? Absurd!

"Have you been hero enough for today?" Priscilla asked.

He did not release her hand as his voice grew cold. "Mayhap *you* have been heroine enough for today, Pris. Why didn't you stop the horse?"

She was about to ask how he thought she could halt a horse; then she heard Mr. Harmsworth speak and realized the question had been for him. He had tossed aside much of his armor. He looked horrified. She could not blame this disaster on anyone but Miss Young.

"I tried to stop the horse as soon as I saw Miss Young on the field. The damn—" Mr. Harmsworth glanced guiltily at her. "The blasted helmet makes it almost impossible to see. I nearly yanked the horse's head off to go around Lady Priscilla."

"But you aimed the lance right at me," she replied, keeping one arm around her son's shoulders. Was Isaac shaking, too, or was it just her reaction?

"Do you think I was going to thrust it through you?" He became a sickly shade of green. Sweat blistered his face. She was unsure if it came from exertion or fear. Putting his foot against the wall, he pulled out the lance and tossed it on the ground. His voice trembled as he said, "I was lifting it to throw it aside, but I was afraid it would strike Miss Young."

She nodded, then wondered if the world was tilting to the side.

"I am sorry to have frightened you, my lady." Mr. Harmsworth glanced at where Dr. Dommel was tending to Miss Young. "I never guessed someone would step in front of our horses."

"Who was riding the other horse?" asked Neville as their host joined them.

He shrugged. "You would have to ask Bennett. He makes those decisions for the actors." Tossing his mail gloves onto the ground, he snarled, "This was an asinine idea."

Lord Stenborough scowled as he kicked aside one of the gloves. "It had a great deal of merit and would have been enjoyable if you had taken care."

"Taken care?" He pushed his face close to the viscount's until Priscilla could not have slid a piece of paper between them. "If you had kept your convenient off the tournament field, my lord, none of this would have happened."

"You are overstepping yourself, Harmsworth. You would be wise to close your mouth before—"

"Before I say that this Faire has been a ridiculous idea?" He turned on his heel and walked away, not slowing even when Lord Stenborough called after him.

The viscount looked at them, and Priscilla knew one of them should say something. She could not imagine what it might be. Aware of her children witnessing the angry exchange, she was relieved when the Reverend Mr. Kenyon hurried up to ask if she was unharmed.

"This must impress upon you, my lord," the vicar

said to Lord Stenborough, "the need to bring an end to any event that might endanger someone."

Lord Stenborough rubbed his hands together, trying to appear distressed. Yet his eyes twinkled as if he were delighted with how the tournament had unfolded. Delighted? That Miss Young had almost allowed herself to be injured or killed?

"Your caution is well taken," the viscount replied. "Although it would have been pleasing for my guests to watch this tournament, I shall bring it to an end."

"Thank you." Reverend Mr. Kenyon's smile was one of relief.

"Our events on the morrow are simple and without a hint of peril." Lord Stenborough's voice rose, so all his guests could hear. "However, each hour will be filled with excitement."

That answer seemed to satisfy the vicar, although Priscilla would have liked to ask more questions. As the viscount invited his guests to join him for refreshments, she frowned.

She put her hand to her head when everything around her seemed to wobble. Bother!

"I think," Neville said quietly, "you need to rest, Pris."

"You may be right." She was not surprised he had taken note of her dizziness. "I am glad the Faire's ball is not tonight, because I doubt I could dance. I have bruised every inch of my dignity." She tried to smile, but winced when he touched the corner of her lip that had been bleeding.

"Let me help you." He wrapped his arm around her waist, and she was glad to lean against his uninjured shoulder. Her left ankle twinged as she walked beside him, and things remained oddly out of focus.

Lord Stenborough shouted something behind

them, but Priscilla did not turn. The sharp sound of his wife's retort made her want to run from the Faire.

"I could use something cold to drink," Neville said as the children bobbed around them, asking dozens of questions Priscilla did not have the energy to answer.

"I believe we all could."

Daphne's nose wrinkled. "Not more of that horrible lemonade, I hope."

"I was thinking of a strong ale." He winked at her.

"Lord Stenborough—"

He interrupted Daphne to say, "I have spent enough time at the Faire for today. Why don't you three go to the tent and see if any of the bottles packed in ice are still cold?"

"Ice?" asked Priscilla when the children hurried toward the brightly striped tent.

"Thanks to Stenborough's ice house." He chuckled. "I am certain our host, if he had given it the least bit of thought, would not mind me taking some of the ice he had put away last winter."

"Thank you."

"For saving you?"

She was more successful at smiling this time. "I was thinking of how you are watching over my children, but, yes, thank you for being my dashing hero this evening."

"'Tis a dashed hard task to be that dashing hero." He touched his shoulder and glowered.

"Is there something I can do to help?"

His frown became a rakish leer. "Your kiss made me feel better before."

Standing on tiptoe, she pressed her lips to his forehead. "You still are too warm."

"You still are close, Pris." He balanced her chin between two fingers. "Why don't you try checking for a fever on my lips rather than my brow?"

"Neville . . ." She glanced back toward where the other guests were leaving the tournament ground.

"You saved Miss Young's life, Pris. Don't fret about her now. Let Dommel attend to her, unless you pine for his company."

"Do not be ludicrous." She dampened her lips, and another sharp sting came from the cracked one. "She is in good hands with the doctor and Lord Stenborough."

He scowled. "Stenborough and that young woman?"

Priscilla told him of Lady Stenborough's comments and Miss Young's reaction. It took longer than she intended because he kept asking questions. She was not sure what he wanted to find out. "Miss Young was so agitated at the idea that Lord Stenborough still cares for his wife enough to make sure she had a good seat for the tournament that she made a silly decision."

"To kill herself? Really, Pris. 'Tis not like you to be dramatic."

"I am not the one being dramatic."

"True, but your supposition is."

"If you believe that, then you explain why she was taking a stroll on the tournament field."

"Mayhap she wanted to put an end to the Faire."

"Or to herself." Priscilla sighed. "I wish someone could make Lord Stenborough see the sense of ending this absurdity."

"And put all these good folks out of work?"

"Actors can always get other jobs."

"Spoken like someone who has never been one."

"*Sir* Neville!" called Orysia.

Priscilla rolled her eyes as the so-called fortune-teller rushed toward them. Orysia was dressed in a brilliant green robe that was decorated with swirls of silver to match the jewels twisted through her hair.

"*Sir* Neville," she continued, in a breathless voice. "I need to speak with you. It is very important."

"It will have to wait." Neville hooked his arm through Priscilla's. "Lady Priscilla needs to be tended to."

"Tended to?" Orysia squinted at her. "What is wrong with you?"

"She is learning that being a hero is not a task for the weakhearted." He chuckled. "Only the weak-headed."

"But I must speak with you!"

"Hathaway!"

Another shout, this one from Lord Stenborough, made Orysia whirl, her lips tilting into a smile. Did she believe the viscount had a *tendre* for her? She must have seen how Lord Stenborough panted after Miss Young's skirt.

Knowing Orysia would not heed her words of caution, Priscilla murmured, "Neville, with the way people are shouting at you, if I were you, I would change my name and not tell anyone what my new name is."

"Not a bad idea," he answered. "Let me see what he wants; then I will get you that drink."

"A drink for me?" Orysia slithered toward him. "*Sir* Neville, I need to talk with you. I saw something disturbing in my cards this afternoon. I fear you will find yourself or someone dear to you in a very heated situation."

"Not now, Orysia."

"You need to listen to me. If—"

"Hathaway!"

Neville shook his head. "Orysia, Lady Priscilla needs to sit for a moment."

"My tent is always open," she cooed.

"I wager that is true," Priscilla said quietly.

Orysia frowned at Priscilla. "What happened to you?"

"I was bumped."

"Come into my tent and sit."

Neville motioned toward the small tent where Orysia was opening the flap. "I shall be only a few moments."

"Really?" Priscilla asked, raising her brows.

"Stenborough *can* be succinct."

"And Orysia *can* tell fortunes."

He grinned. "Your point is well taken. I will be back as soon as I can. If you see Bennett, ask him who was riding the other horse."

"Please ask how Miss Young fares."

"A dangerous task when she seems to feel she owes me a duty for saving her."

"'Tis that Hathaway charm. It sends young women swooning."

"Spare me such faux compliments."

"What makes you believe they are false?"

His laugh was terse. "Stay here and sit quietly."

Priscilla acquiesced. Her head ached, her side ached, and her ankle twinged each time she took a step. Sitting seemed like an excellent idea.

"This way," Orysia said, smiling as she came back to where Priscilla stood.

She was astonished when Orysia led her into the tent. Its interior was as opulent as Orysia's costume. What appeared to be silk was draped to hide the canvas. The thick scent of musky incense was smothering. Pillows were heaped in a corner, reminiscent of the ones in Neville's tent. A single brass lamp hung, unlit, from the roof's peak.

"Here," urged Orysia, pointing to a simple chair.

"Thank you." As she lowered herself with care, each bruise battled for her attention.

Orysia rearranged her robes as she sat on the other side of the table lost beneath a swath of yellow silk. She pulled a pack of cards from beneath the table.

Priscilla frowned. "Please do not offer to read my future."

"You do not want me to know?" Orysia grinned, not appearing insulted.

"Why would I want to know what is going to happen? I cannot halt it."

Orysia laughed, and her kohl-lined eyes widened. "You are not interested in the future of your heart?"

"I trust it will be beating for many years to come."

"Your health is not what I speak of."

Priscilla nodded. She had known that was not what Orysia meant. How appealing was the idea of discovering if the affection growing between her and Neville would continue into the future. And how deluding.

"I do not believe it would be wise for me to take part in these games," she said. "My late husband was a parson, and it is not appropriate for me to pretend you can read my future with cards."

"Pretend?" Orysia scowled. "I do not pretend, my lady."

"Do you know who usually rides in the tournament for your troupe?"

She preened. "Of course. I know as much about this troupe as Bennett does."

"Who was riding the other horse today?"

"Burr."

"With his injured leg?"

Orysia rolled her painted eyes. "My dear Lady Priscilla, we do not have the luxury of waiting for our wounds to heal. We must work. Give me your hands."

"Excuse me."

"Give me your hands."

Priscilla started to stand, then paused when her head began to ache anew. Arguing was pointless. She might as well give in and get this over with.

Orysia grabbed Priscilla's hands and tilted them toward the faint light. Except for one, her nails were all long and pointed. "I need to see both. One tells me what you were born with, and the other what will come. Which interests you more?"

Struggling not to laugh, Priscilla said, "I know what I was born with. My children or my friends will be glad to give you a list of my shortcomings."

"Then let us see what will come." When Orysia twisted her palms to a strange angle, Priscilla saw that her right elbow was scraped beneath her torn sleeve. No wonder it burned as much as her lip.

She listened while Orysia mumbled to herself. Was this all the actress did? If so, Priscilla was unimpressed. Scraping her tongue across her sore lip, she wished Neville would hurry back. That was a fruitless hope, because she had never heard Lord Stenborough use one word when he could use a score.

Orysia's voice became low and husky. "I see danger here."

"Do you?"

She frowned. "You do not sound concerned, Lady Priscilla."

"Why should I be? *I* see danger at the Faire, and I am not a fortune-teller."

"But did you know of the danger focused on you?"

"Mayhap I should take my leave in the morning, as I have planned."

"That would be wise." Orysia's long nail jabbed at Priscilla's palm. "Here is a turn for good luck. It appears it will be soon. Are you expecting good tidings?"

Priscilla forced a smile. If she tried, she could make each of Orysia's oblique comments fit some aspect of her life. When she heard Neville's voice, she jerked her hand away. She yelped as the fortune-teller's talon scratched her palm. Excusing herself, she went outside.

"Neville," she said, "thank you for—Constable Forshaw!"

His face was set in its sternest lines. "Lady Priscilla, I need to speak with you and Sir Neville. Now."

She looked at Neville. His expression was as grim as the constable's.

"How long have you been gone from the tournament grounds?" the constable asked.

"Not long. Half an hour, maybe a little less," she replied, again glancing at Neville.

"Where have you been since then?"

"Here with Orysia Aleksandovicheva."

At her name, Orysia poked her head out of the tent. "What is it? Who are you?"

"Constable Forshaw," he answered tersely.

"Why are you asking these questions?" asked Priscilla.

Instead of answering, he said, "I understand

Garvin Harmsworth almost rode you down, my lady."

"It was an accident. I was trying——"

"I understand as well that Mr. Harmsworth and Sir Neville exchanged angry words afterward."

"Angry?" Priscilla smiled. "To own the truth, Constable Forshaw, Neville was furious at all of us." She wished Neville would speak. It was unlike him to remain silent. "What has happened?"

"We just found Garvin Harmsworth and the lad Burr. They are dead."

TWELVE

Priscilla did not argue when Neville refused to let her go into the tent at the edge of the tournament field. When he told her that Mr. Harmsworth had died with a dagger in his chest and young Burr had been stabbed in the back, her stomach ached. Mayhap Duncan had been lucky. He had escaped alive.

"This is unbelievable," moaned Orysia. She drew her scarf over her face as her shoulders shook.

Priscilla wanted to agree. The lad had been struck by an arrow and had gamely continued with his work. Now he and Mr. Harmsworth were dead. Both riders in the tournament, but why?

"You saw no one out of the ordinary?" asked the constable.

The bizarre yearning to laugh was not easy to smother, but Priscilla said, "Look around you, Constable Forshaw. Everything here is out of the ordinary."

Neville asked, "Could it be a murder and a suicide, Constable?"

"Suicide." Constable Forshaw tapped his chin. "It is always possible, but why would Harmsworth kill the lad and then himself?"

"His employer and friends would know better than we would."

"The wisest thing would be to cancel the Faire," Priscilla added.

"Lady Priscilla," said Constable Forshaw with a sigh, "if you can coax Lord Stenborough to do that, I would be deeply grateful."

"Can't you order it ended?"

"This is not Stonehall-on-Sea, my lady. I can only suggest to the viscount that he reconsider his plans."

"Three men are dead, one more injured. How much more does he need to have happen before he ends this?"

"You must ask him, my lady."

"This is beneath reproach. If this murderer believes he will not be caught after killing—again—what stops him from murdering once more?"

Constable Forshaw looked rather bleak.

"Pris, calm yourself."

She bristled at Neville's serene voice. "I will when this murderer is caught. If this was not a murder and a suicide but instead two murders, then—"

Constable Forshaw's forehead knit as his brows bent toward each other. "Mayhap the coroner's investigation will tell us that. Until then, we should not make any assumptions."

"And who will die while we wait for Mr. Semple's report?"

"It is not like you to be in a panic, Lady Priscilla."

"I am not in a panic." She stepped closer to Neville, wishing he would put his arm around her. As shadows closed down around the Faire, it was too easy to imagine that each held a lurking murderer. "I am frightened."

With a shout, Lord Stenborough rushed toward them with all the speed he could muster. His face was flushed in the day's last light. "Constable Forshaw, you are here! It is horrible! So horrible. All that blood! Who would have guessed he would do something like this?"

"We thought you might have that answer," Neville said.

"Why would I?" He frowned at each of them in turn. "Harmsworth was my employee, but I know little about him other than his skills as an estate manager. I shall be hard-pressed to find another as competent."

"Mayhap if you ask some of your guests for a recommendation . . ." Neville's smile was icy.

"Guests?" He turned to the constable. "You must keep this quiet."

"How do you think this can be kept quiet, Stenborough?" Neville asked.

"He is correct," said Constable Forshaw. "Gentlemen, if you please." He motioned to his right.

Priscilla fought the instinct to bristle at being left out of another conversation, but she nodded when Neville squeezed her hand and gave her a bolstering smile. She would go to comfort her children and aunt. First thing in the morning, they would return to Stonehall-on-Sea.

From beyond the fake castle that was unsettlingly crimson in the light being strained through thickening clouds, the cheerful sounds of the Faire continued. Lord Stenborough refused to bring the Faire to an end. Neville's silence added to her exasperation. She recalled Constable Forshaw's interest in Neville's whereabouts at the time of Mr. Harmsworth's death, but Neville was not staying silent to protect himself. She could give him an alibi. There must be something else.

"Who would have guessed the estate manager

would kill poor Burr and himself?" asked Orysia, gazing toward where Lord Stenborough stood in tense conversation with Neville and the constable. Her mouth tightened when Lord Stenborough glanced at her and quickly away before he walked toward the castle. Her smile returned, brittle and strained. "Do you think he did it so Burr could not speak up against him for nearly running you and the other woman down?"

More sharply than she had intended, Priscilla asked, "Does that mean you did not see any of this in your cards?"

"I only look into the future for my patrons. Mr. Harmsworth did not believe in my skills with the cards. He made fun of me. He made fun of lots of people."

Priscilla clenched her hands. She suspected Orysia knew more about this than she had revealed.

"I thought he was pleasant," Priscilla said.

Orysia's full lips twisted. "That is because you did not have to work for him. I should not say this, but I am not surprised he killed himself."

"I do not think he did."

"You really think he was murdered?" Her face paled beneath thick layers of rice powder.

"Someone is stalking people at this Faire, killing at will."

"Do not say that. It is too horrible to think about." She pulled a deck of cards from her bodice and shuffled them.

Priscilla watched her slender hands. Orysia was frightened, too. Mayhap the actress was smarter than she had thought. Priscilla wished Orysia was truly able to see the future. Then she would be able to give them a glimmer of the murderer's identity.

Had Mr. Harmsworth been made to look like someone with the opportunity to murder before he was killed by the real murderer? That made no sense, and that was what terrified her. Someone was treating the Faire like a private hunting preserve, making all of them fair game. But who? Who had killed the actor Roland and the boy Burr and Mr. Harmsworth? Who had tried to kill Duncan? Had the first attack on Burr been an accident? Too many questions, too many people, and absolutely no answers.

A shadow crossed Orysia's fingers, and Priscilla looked up to see Lady Stenborough. Distaste pulled at Orysia's mouth, creating an expression similar to Miss Young's in the pavilion. What had Lady Stenborough done to infuriate the fortune-teller?

"Can you believe this?" demanded Lady Stenborough. "First the attack at the banquet grounds. Now this!"

"Calm yourself," Orysia ordered. "Getting into a miff will not help anything."

Lady Stenborough glared, then seemed to realize she might be infuriating a woman she believed had mystical powers. Wiping her brow with a lacy handkerchief that had been dipped in heavy perfume, the scent of which threatened to overpower Priscilla, she sighed. "My poor, dear husband. This is such a strain on him. Thank goodness I am here. He needs his loving wife at a time like this."

Orysia made a strangled sound before rushing back into her tent. She dropped the flap behind her.

Lady Stenborough continued as if Orysia had never been there. "I know *you* will understand, Lady Priscilla. You are not like the actors. We have never had such bad luck."

"I should hope not!"

"Lady Priscilla, you cannot blame Stenborough Park for this misfortune. The Faire is surely an innocent target."

Priscilla wondered how Lady Stenborough could be such a complete block. Of course the Faire was the target. There was no other connection between Duncan McAndrews, Garvin Harmsworth, and the two actors who had been killed.

"If you could entreat your husband to bring the Faire to an end—"

"No!" The deeper voice came from behind Lady Stenborough.

Priscilla sighed when Lord Stenborough came up beside his wife. Arguing with him herself would be fruitless. Mayhap if she left the couple to discuss this, Lady Stenborough would be able to show her husband the wisdom of cutting short his birthday celebration.

"I thought you," Lord Stenborough said, "would have sympathy for me, Lady Priscilla."

"Sympathy for you?" She stared at him, astonished. Was Lord Stenborough being honest or was he lying to protect himself? If that were so, she did not want to think what he would do to keep the truth from being exposed. Telling herself she was being silly, for the man seldom had a thought worthy of being voiced, she added, "Sympathy for what? You have not been attacked with a bow or a dagger."

"Would you like to spend your birthday being interrogated by the constable?"

She could not think of a thing to say, for her shock was too great. The viscount acted less mature than her son, pouting because his party had not gone as he wished.

"Edwin, do not badger her!" snapped Lady Stenborough. "How can you expect her to share our distress about what has happened with our plans for the Faire?"

Priscilla had to leave before she said something she would regret—mayhap. Bidding them a good evening, she hobbled toward the tent where the children would be waiting. When she heard the Stenboroughs firing recriminations at each other, she was glad she had taken her leave.

The laughter coming from the tent welcomed Priscilla inside. She held out her arms and was nearly bowled over by her children's enthusiastic greetings.

"Where is Aunt Cordelia?" she asked when she saw they were the only ones in the tent.

"She went to pay Mr. McAndrews a visit."

"At this hour?" She looked outside to see the sun had vanished behind the manor house. "You must be hungry."

"Starved!" announced Isaac, his grin returning. "Can we eat here?"

She shook her head. She wanted them within the walls of Stenborough Park before dark, although she wondered if that would imperil her children more. It was possible the murderer was among the guests seeking sanctuary in the manor house.

"Shall we go to our rooms and see what sort of lovely tea Lady Stenborough has arranged for us?" she asked, trying to sound as cheerful as the music from the Faire.

Leah hung back when her older sister and younger brother went to the house. "Mama?"

"Yes?" She put her arm around her daughter's slim shoulders.

"Jaspar said we should leave straightaway. He said

many of the actors are planning to be gone by morning."

Priscilla had to search her mind before she realized Leah was speaking of the young man she had met at the Faire. Jaspar must be a member of the acting troupe. "I think your friend is wise. We will be leaving in the morning, too."

"Really?" She smiled. "I am glad, Mama, that we and Aunt Cordelia and Uncle Neville will be safe."

"Neville may not be leaving." She would not be false with her daughter.

"But he must, Mama! I don't want him getting hurt."

"Neither do I. However, I don't believe he will leave Stenborough Park until Mr. McAndrews is able to travel."

Leah nodded. She knew, as Priscilla did, that Neville would not leave a friend in danger.

Rain pattered through the windows by the time Priscilla and the children reached their apartment. Closing all but one window, which she left open a bit for air, she tried to reassure the children that Neville would be fine. It was impossible when she could not be certain herself.

She was pleased—and not a little surprised—that Isaac was as agreeable as Leah to the idea of leaving on the morrow. Even Daphne, who hungered for any chance to be among the *ton*, eager for the time when she could be fired off, was sensible.

Tea was brought with a collection of sandwiches and sweets. When she saw an extra pot of hot water, she guessed this was the kitchen's way of telling them to eat well because there would be no supper. Isaac ate as if he had not in months, but he was the only one. Leah and Daphne put food on their plates, yet hardly tasted it. Priscilla did not indulge in the hypocrisy of pretending she could eat. Her stomach roiled as too many appalling thoughts flashed through her head.

She stood by the window, stepping back when lightning flashed, turning the trees into black silhouettes against the bright sky. Through the storm, she could see people hurrying to shelter. Most of the tents sagged beneath the rain puddling on them, and she wondered how many would last the night.

"Uncle Neville!" she heard Isaac shout.

She turned to face the door, envying him as he ran to throw himself in Neville's embrace. She wanted to be within those strong arms. She watched him hug each of her children and say something that brought tentative smiles. Then they stepped back, and he raised his arms. She did not hesitate as she let them enfold her. She pressed her face to his unhurt shoulder, drawing in a deep scent of him, so alive. His heartbeat was a muted reminder that her worst fears had not been realized. He was safe.

Raising her head, she steered his mouth to hers. She needed to kiss him as she never had before. When she moaned as even his gentle kiss hurt her cracked lip, he drew back and framed her face with his hands.

"Pris, don't be frightened on my behalf," he murmured.

"Why not? You are the most foolhardy person I know. You will rush in not only where angels fear to tread, but where the devil is scared to go."

"You are right. I have trod where the devil has been." He sighed, abruptly looking exhausted and like a man who had suffered a wound only hours before.

Even though she wanted to remain close to him, his hands touching her, connecting them in a way they had only begun to explore, Priscilla edged away. She smiled at her children before saying, "Please take the rest of your tea into your rooms. I will come to tuck you in before you go to sleep."

Again she thought Daphne might protest, but her oldest steered the other children out of the room as soon as Isaac had heaped his plate once more. She smiled sadly. Once they were safely back in Stone-hall-on-Sea, she would arrange for some sort of treat to make up for what they had missed at Stenborough Park.

"You have good, sensible children, Pris," Neville said.

She closed the door behind Isaac, then came back to where Neville still stood. "They are scared. They are afraid we are going to be the next victims."

"It is possible."

"What?"

He held out a slip of paper. "Look at this."

She read aloud, "'Thou know'st 'tis common; all that live must die, Passing through nature to eternity.' Oh, sweet heavens."

"My thoughts exactly, although my language was a bit more forceful and far less dignified."

"Do you know what it means?"

"It is from *Hamlet*. Act One, Scene Two," he said as he took it. He flashed her a challenging grin. "Do not grimace. I did not waste my years in the theater on witless comedies and melodramas."

"But what do you think it means?"

"In this context, I believe it means Harmsworth was murdered."

"I agree. Unless . . . Do you recognize the handwriting as his?"

"It isn't. Lord Stenborough confirmed that." He turned the page over. It was blank. "I doubt there is much else we can derive from it."

"Except that Mr. Harmsworth definitely did not commit suicide. This does not sound like a suicide note left by a man in despair at having murdered another."

"I suspect you are right, just as I suspect he did not know Hamlet from ham and eggs."

"So this may not be the last murder."

His voice was taut. "I think you are right about that, too."

Priscilla almost wished he had lied to her. She sat and poured a cup of tea for him, adding some lemon. She held it out as she asked, "What does Constable Forshaw think of this?"

"He is not certain, especially when the murder scene has all the trappings of a suicide." He took the cup and sipped before sitting beside her.

"Ignoring the note for the moment, what possible reason would Mr. Harmsworth have for killing himself?"

"He was distraught over—"

"Why do people always say 'distraught' at times like this?"

"Because it is the right word, Pris. Harmsworth was *distraught* over Roland's murder. Such emotions have been known to cause a person to end his or her own life."

"True, but Mr. Harmsworth does not—" She shivered again as she corrected herself. "Mr. Harmsworth did not seem like someone who would commit suicide. He seemed enthusiastic about the Faire and other plans."

"Mayhap he did not want you to know about his *real* plans. He was suffering from uncertainty when we visited him in the tent before the tournament."

"Of course he was uneasy. He was about to joust for the first time with a young man who had done it often. I am sure Harmsworth was hoping he would suffer no more than some bruises. I cannot believe he would kill himself. Was there a suicide note in addition to this quote from Shakespeare?"

"No, but mayhap he did not have anything to say." He picked up his tea and took a sip.

"You have a lot of mayhaps. Don't you think it is time for you to say something definite instead of more conjecture?"

"Blast it, Pris! I am as confounded as you with this puzzle that seems to have no answer." His voice became as grim as his expression. "All right. I will say something definite. It *is* time for me to put aside conjecture, because I don't know how much time any of us has left."

THIRTEEN

Priscilla came back out into the antechamber after wishing her children a good night's rest. She hoped they were not plagued with nightmares that skulked into their sleep.

Neville had taken off his ruined coat, leaving it on the floor beside where he sat. His face was almost the shade of his white shirt, where it was not stained hideously with his blood. He was eating a piece of cake.

She crossed the room and picked up a sandwich, taking one bite before putting it back down. How could she swallow when her throat closed each time she saw that dried blood on him? She was not squeamish. Rather, she was unsettled to realize how easily he could have been killed. Then . . . She had no idea what she would have done then. She had survived Lazarus's death and emerged from her mourning ready to embrace life again. She was not sure she could endure losing another man who had such an important place in her heart.

"I am sorry, Pris," Neville said, startling her out of her sad thoughts.

"Sorry? About what?"

"What I said earlier. Scaring you more is stupid."

She walked behind the chair that faced the settee

he was seated on and folded her arms on its back. Neville had not come to his feet when she came back into the room, and she guessed his shoulder was paining him.

"Don't be sorry for speaking honestly." She tried to smile. "If everyone else was as forthright, we would know who killed those men."

"And if wishes were horses, beggars would ride."

She came around the chair and put her hand against his forehead. It was cooler than it had been earlier.

"What is that for?" he asked.

"I thought you might be sickening when your only response was a nursery rhyme." She took his hand between hers. "Neville, I want you to go with us in the morning."

"Go? I cannot leave when Duncan is still too weak to be moved, and Constable Forshaw needs my help."

"You will be no help if you are the next victim."

"Me?" His dark eyes narrowed. "Who has been filling your head with pap, Pris?"

"No one. I have been trying to make this whole jumble fit into a rational pattern. Duncan has very dark hair. Mr. Harmsworth had very dark hair. So do you."

"Roland had dark hair as well."

She nodded. "See what I mean?"

"Many of the other men here have dark hair."

"You all are of a similar age."

"Mayhap, but it still fails to make a pattern." He shook his head. "How could the murderer have known that Duncan was going to be at the banquet then?"

Sitting, she said, "Anyone who knew Duncan was

calling on you would have guessed he would come here with you."

Neville opened his mouth, then closed it. His brow rutted with thought. "That is true."

"And who knew Duncan was with you in Town?"

"Me."

She smiled when he did. "True, but I believe we can say you were not the archer because you were with me when the quarrels were fired. Who else?"

"Stenborough could have known." He laughed shortly. "He had to know. Duncan received an invitation, too."

"But what reason would Stenborough have to slay Duncan and the others? If they were leaving him a bequest in their wills, it would make sense."

Neville regarded her intently. "What have you heard, Pris?"

She shared with him what Lady Stenborough had said about paying for the Faire out of her dower.

"So Stenborough is at *point non plus*, is he?" He considered that for a moment. "That may have some bearing on this, or none at all. We are getting nowhere."

"Mayhap Constable Forshaw will come up with something."

"Anything is possible." He grimaced. "Blast this shoulder."

"You should have the doctor examine it again."

"Don't nag, Pris."

"I am not nagging." She reached toward the bandaging. When he growled like a hurt dog, she ignored him.

"Stop, Pris, or I shall send for Dr. Dommel."

"You know how to threaten someone to get your way, don't you?" She shrugged. "It could wait until morning as long as you curb your natural instincts to jump into the midst of a fight. But as I believe that is impossible—"

Priscilla was glad when he did not retort. With care, she began to untie the bandage. No further signs of fresh blood were visible, which was good. When he groaned, she handed him a cup of tea.

"It will have to do," she said. "I have nothing stronger here."

He set the cup back on the tray. "Pris, I have been thinking about something."

"What is that?"

"I have been thinking about how bothered you are by Dommel's less-than-subtle hints that you should welcome his calls."

Seeing some dried blood on the bandaging, she loosened it more carefully. She lifted off the last of it and dropped it onto the floor. The wound was not festering, which pleased her. "No more bothered than you are by Miss Young's sudden worship of you as her dashing hero since she awoke in your arms on the tournament grounds."

"My point exactly."

She paused. "And what point is that?"

"These flirtations are becoming annoying." He took her hand and held it between his. "I was wondering if you would be interested in a betrothal."

"A betrothal?" she breathed. She must have heard him wrong. Neville had disdained the idea of marriage for as long as she had known him. He had stated many times that he believed Priscilla and Lazarus's happy marriage had been an aberration.

She saw the entreaty in his eyes. As he stroked her fingers, she wanted to succumb to the tingles of anticipation flowing through her. She yearned for him to draw her to him, her lips against his. In his arms, she was sure she could find ecstasy.

"A betrothal of convenience," he said softly.

"A what?" She drew back, waiting for his laugh. To her amazement, she saw no humor in his expression.

"A betrothal of convenience. A betrothal that would serve a purpose for both of us without being a real one. It would be much the same as a marriage of convenience, just without the pastor's involvement."

"Now, Neville, I don't know what you have in mind, but I will not do anything that will reflect poorly on my children."

He winced as he moved his left shoulder. When she chided him as she began to dab at the crusted blood with a cloth dipped into the water in a second teapot, he said, "Such an arrangement will reflect less poorly on them than the games of cat-and-mouse we are forced to play with Dommel and Miss Young."

"Aha!"

"Pris, don't say 'aha' in that superior tone. It cannot be a secret I am eager to put some distance between me and the marriage-minded Miss Young. Mayhap she will return her attentions to Stenborough when she realizes her hopes for me taking her to Town are futile." He cursed as she continued to clean the wound. Without an apology for his language, he added, "And I know you are as desirous of giving Dommel his *congé*. What better way to do both?"

"You are diabolical."

"So does that mean you will say yes?"

"To a betrothal of convenience?"

He nodded.

"Give me a moment to consider this unexpected offer."

"I thought you would give me an enthusiastic yes. Mayhap Dommel is not as bothersome as it appears."

"Or as bothersome as Miss Young is for you?"

He gave her a grim smile. "I have been trying to be polite when speaking of her. What do you say, Pris?"

"As I said, give me a moment to consider this most unexpected offer." She picked up another napkin and ripped it into strips. She would use them to re-bandage his shoulder. She poured water from the extra teapot into a low bowl so she could lather the material to his arm. As she turned to wrap the bandaging around his arm, she froze. She could only watch in silence while he stood and peeled off his bloodstained shirt.

She stared. No, she was not staring. She was gawking as Aunt Cordelia would have chided Daphne and Leah not to do. She wanted to pull her gaze away, but it was riveted on his bare chest. Even as she reminded herself that she had been a pastor's wife and had sat at the bedside of many ailing parishioners—both female and male—and seen such an expanse of skin before, she could not keep from admiring the firm muscles that had pressed against her each time he drew her close.

Her fingers quivered in a wordless request to let them glide along his skin. Quivered too much, she realized, when water splashed from the bowl onto her shoes.

"Do you need help with that, Pris?" Neville asked.

The very serenity of his question vexed her. Here he was parading about like a cyprian, and yet he acted as if everything remained just as it had always been.

"Do you have everything you need?" He tossed the shirt atop the discarded bandaging.

She almost told him yes, for this man who exasperated her as no other ever had was slipping more deeply into her heart. She must not be an air dreamer. This would be the worst time to be addled.

"If you will sit, I shall tend to your shoulder." Her voice was a bit too clipped, but she could not take back the words now.

His eyes narrowed again as he sat. "Pris, if my offer of a betrothal of convenience has offended you, you are welcome to ignore it or scold me or stamp out of the room in a pelter."

"I am not offended by your offer." Kneeling, she put the bowl and bandaging beside him.

"You are offended by something." He yelped when she dabbed at his shoulder again. When she hushed him, not wanting to draw the children out of their rooms, he said, "Be careful."

"Advice you should have taken for yourself, and then you would not be in this predicament."

His hand cupped her chin, raising her face up toward his.

"Neville," she whispered, "let me bandage this."

Instead of answering, he ran his thumb along her jaw. Her fingers curled around his forearm. She was unsure whether she intended to push him away or bring him nearer. She could not trust her thoughts. Too many conflicting ones cavorted through her head.

"Pris, am *I* upsetting you?"

She was about to fire back an answer at him, then faltered when her gaze was captured by his. Knowing he was waiting for an answer—an *honest* answer—she leaned toward him, unable to resist the invitation in his dark eyes.

A scream exploded through the night. Priscilla pulled back, bumping the dish of water. It splattered over her and Neville. Another shriek rose like a clap of thunder, turning her knees to India rubber. Her heart pounded in her ears as she rushed to the door.

"No!" Neville caught her and pushed her aside even as he struggled to pull on his shirt. He reached for his coat. "Stay here."

When screams sounded again, she asked, "How do you know *here* is safe?"

He frowned at her. "We have had this discussion already."

"Then why are we wasting time having it again?"

"Why do you have to be so blasted logical?"

As yet another shriek careened through the night, setting every fiber of her being on edge, Priscilla ran after Neville. Servants milled about in the hallways and at the base of the staircase. Neville pushed through them, and she followed before the servants could huddle back together in fear.

Rain pelted her when she emerged from the house, and lightning burst from the clouds. Neville turned toward the wagons where the troupe was staying. She tried to follow, but her feet slipped on the wet grass. Before she could tumble, he caught her.

"Go!" she ordered. "I will keep up as best as I can."

"You always do the best you can." He squeezed her hand before running toward the wagons at a pace she could not match.

The screams began again, and her nails cut into her palms as she clenched her hands. Who was screaming?

"Over there!" she called, although there was no one

nearby to hear her shout. She pointed toward a wagon with its door thrown open. Light blazed from it.

Other forms appeared from the darkness. One of them collapsed. The cries halted in the middle of a screech.

Priscilla dropped to her knees beside the prone form. "'Tis Orysia!" she gasped.

"Is she dead?" she heard someone shout.

Neville ran over and knelt next to her, lifting Orysia's arm to check her pulse. "Not dead. She has fainted." With a wry grin, he hefted the woman into his arms.

"Neville, watch your shoulder!"

"I will leave that task to you. C'mon."

"Where are you taking her?"

"To that tent, which has a lamp lit."

Priscilla jumped to her feet. She grimaced as mud dripped from her skirt, but hurried to the tent. She flung open the flap and stared at the three people within. Miss Young was holding her wrapper close to her chin as she watched Lord Stenborough and his wife arguing. As they stared at Priscilla, Lady Stenborough's accusing screech hung in the air. It must have drowned out Orysia's screams.

"Lady Priscilla, what—what are you doing here?" choked Lord Stenborough.

She wanted to ask the same as she stepped aside to let Neville enter. Hearing Lady Stenborough's choked gasp and Miss Young's moan of despair, Priscilla left the flap open, not caring who else came in.

Neville put the senseless woman on the bed in the cramped tent. It was much smaller than any of the tents he had brought, and the roof was lower. When Priscilla backed out of the way, her head brushed the canvas. Within, however, it was as elegant as the

finest house on Berkeley Square. The bed was wide
and topped with what appeared to be a silk coverlet.
Lamps glowed brightly on mahogany tables set on
an elegant carpet atop boards to prevent it from getting wet. The most outrageous item was a fancy
writing desk with a fragile-looking chair beside it.

Lord Stenborough lurched toward the bed and
grabbed the footboard. He stared at Orysia, horror
lining his face and adding years to it. "She isn't dead,
is she?" He grasped Neville by the shoulders.

Neville knocked his hands away, wincing. "Calm
yourself, Stenborough. No, you don't have another
corpse."

"What happened to her? Orysia, can you answer
me?"

Priscilla frowned as she looked from the frantic
man to his wife. Lady Stenborough was staring, confusion stealing the fury from her face. Behind her,
Miss Young wore a similar expression. Not that she
could fault them for being amazed at the viscount's
dismay at what had happened to an actress he probably had met only once before—where the troupe
had previously performed.

"Pris," Neville asked, "can you find a damp cloth?"

She was tempted to laugh, because everything
around them was damp—except for the fury between Lady Stenborough and Miss Young. Paying it
no mind, she shoved past the viscount and his wife.

Picking up a chemise that was tossed onto the
floor, she dunked it into a pail of water just outside
the tent. She came back to the bed. She had to edge
around the Stenboroughs, who had not moved.
Lord Stenborough backed away, looked at his wife,
and then went to stand by the bottom of the bed so
he could watch Orysia regain her senses.

"Everyone needs to leave," Priscilla said as she bent to wipe mud from Orysia's face. When Neville seconded the command, the sound of grumbled protests told her that no one intended to obey.

Orysia's dark eyelashes fluttered. She stared about in confusion. Her eyes widened when her gaze met Priscilla's. Then they swept the room, narrowing as she noted Lady Stenborough and Miss Young beyond the bed. She looked last at Lord Stenborough. She released the breath she must have been holding, and a wobbly smile appeared and vanished so swiftly Priscilla wondered if she had been mistaken in thinking she had seen it.

When Orysia started to sit up, Priscilla put her hands on the fortune-teller's slim shoulders. Without her fancy robes and heavy cosmetics, Orysia appeared delicate. As delicate as the balance of terror at the Faire.

Priscilla shook herself. She must not surrender to fear.

"What happened?" Orysia moaned, then answered her own question. "I remember. He tried to kill me."

"Kill you?"

Before Orysia could answer, Neville asked, "Why were you out in the storm?"

"I was not taking a walk." Her narrow lips tightened. "I had finished arranging my tent for tomorrow's readings and was going to my wagon." Again she moaned. "I should not have gone into my wagon. *He* was there."

"Who was there?"

Orysia's wide eyes filled with tears. "I don't know. A tall man was tearing through my costumes. They are in shreds." She pulled something out of her pocket. The sheer scarf was not much bigger than a

man's handkerchief. "Look! I snatched this from
him. It has been ripped to pieces." She shuddered,
sitting up. "Thank you for coming to my rescue,
Lady Priscilla. If not for you, I would be dead."

"You cannot be sure of that," Neville argued.
"Mayhap he simply wished to frighten you."

"That is right." When Lord Stenborough seconded the comment, Priscilla flinched. She had not
realized he had moved so close to her.

Orysia put her hands to her neck. "If you do not
believe me, look here." Pulling back her high collar, she pointed to a red welt across her throat. "He
tried to strangle me. I pulled away. When I
screamed, he tried to catch me. I ran. He caught me
again, but I kept screaming."

"Who was it?"

Her luminous eyes focused on Neville. "I do not
know. I could not see him clearly."

"Describe what you could see. You said he was tall.
There is a lamp burning in your wagon. You must
have seen something."

She lowered her eyes. "I don't want to remember,
but I cannot forget. He had wide hands with long
fingers. He was tall. Very tall. The light was so dim
that I could not see well. His hair might have been
blond or gray. I don't recall anything else. I was too
scared."

Priscilla sighed. Orysia's description could fit almost any light-haired man attending the Faire.
When she heard a moan, she put her hand under
Lady Stenborough's elbow and eased her onto Miss
Young's desk chair. When Stenborough patted his
wife's shoulder, she suspected they had temporarily
set aside their quarrel.

Quarrel? She tried to square her shoulders in defiance of her own thoughts. It was impossible to banish them when even a commonplace word brought forth the horror.

Miss Young crossed her arms in front of her, scowling as angrily as Orysia had. Was she upset that her tryst with the viscount had been interrupted twice? Or was she scared?

Into the silence, Priscilla said, "I do not think Orysia needs a doctor, but you had better send for Constable Forshaw."

"No, that is not necessary," Orysia said quickly, drawing everyone's attention to her. "As long as *he* does not come back, I shall be fine."

"You need to rest."

"How could I rest in my wagon?"

"Mayhap Miss Young will not object to you staying here tonight," Neville suggested. "What do you say, Miss Young?"

She blinked several times, then said, "I would not be so coarse as to ask her to leave. I—" She wobbled.

Neville put his arm around her waist, then flexed the fingers on his left hand. Priscilla had been right when she warned him not to strain his shoulder. But he could not leave Orysia senseless in the mud.

"Thank you," Miss Young said. She looked up with a smile he would have labeled coy under other circumstances. Of all the nonsense! How could she be thinking of playing the coquette with him when Orysia had been attacked? More important, how could she act so when her lover was watching? Mayhap she hoped to make Stenborough so jealous that he would toss aside his wife and take Miss Young to Town posthaste.

"You are welcome."

"And you are very kind," she said in a breathy voice that suggested they were alone.

He saw Lord Stenborough's frown and Priscilla's grin. Trust her to guess how Miss Young was taking advantage of this situation.

"Stenborough," he said as he shifted enough so that Miss Young's leg was not rubbing his. Under other circumstances, he would have found a way—a somewhat gentle way or stronger if she did not accept the truth—to remind her that Stenborough was her target, not Neville Hathaway. Mayhap Miss Young was trying to make the viscount jealous enough to toss aside his wife, but Neville had no interest in becoming a part of what could easily become a shocking mull that would keep tongues wagging for days.

"Stenborough," he began again, "let me make sure the intruder has left."

"All right," grumbled Stenborough. Looking at Orysia, who was watching intently, he said, "I will stay here and watch over these ladies."

"If you will sit here, Miss Young . . ." Neville untangled himself from her arms—how many did she have? There seemed to be more than two—and sat her back on the foot of the bed.

"Thank you," she whispered, aiming her warm breath at his ear. "You are so brave. You will be here tomorrow night for the birthday masquerade, won't you? I hope you do not believe me forward to say I would be delighted to have you as my escort."

"That will not be possible," Neville said.

"Oh . . . Why is it not possible?"

Priscilla slipped her hand onto Neville's arm and said in an overly sweet tone, "Because Sir Neville and

I are planning to announce our betrothal at the masquerade tomorrow evening."

While stunned silence filled the tent, Neville smiled at Priscilla. Trust her to come to his rescue against this overly anxious miss who wanted to use him to force her lover's hand. When she smiled back, he cupped her chin and kissed her lightly. There *were* some advantages to this feigned betrothal, such as being able to show such signs of affection while among others. He wondered why he had not considered those advantages before.

He accepted congratulations from their host and his wife. Miss Young was deflated, quite humiliated. He regretted that, but she had forced his hand. He almost chuckled aloud. To own the truth, Miss Young had forced Priscilla's hand. For that, he had to be grateful.

He bid good night to Miss Young and Orysia, who was smiling as broadly at the announced betrothal as if she were the one who intended to marry. On the morrow, he was sure the fortune-teller would be telling everyone how she had seen this in her cards.

As he went to the open flap, he held out his hand. "Coming, Pris?"

Rain struck his face as he stepped out of the tent. It was raining harder than it had been before. A crowd, which must have been waiting for someone to appear, pressed forward. He waved them away with a clipped explanation that there was nothing to worry about.

"You are lying," Priscilla murmured as they continued toward the manor house.

"Or I am telling the truth."

She sneezed and wiped rain from her eyes as he

hurried her toward the house. "Do you think her story is nothing but a drama she created?"

"Yes."

"But why?"

"Haven't you noticed that Orysia seems to be around whenever anyone else becomes the focus of attention? Then she does something to bring that attention back to her."

She was silent for the length of several heartbeats, then said, "You are right. But what reason could she have had to create a scene tonight?"

"She could have heard the brangle in Miss Young's tent from her wagon. Mayhap she wanted to be part of the excitement."

"How bizarre! I wonder what else she might do?"

"I don't think you need to worry. I presume the screams and incriminations will be forgotten by everyone in the wake of your announcement of our betrothal." He paused in the doorway to the house, glad to be out of the rain, and looked back to see the guests in small groups. They were talking with excitement and gesturing in the direction he and Priscilla had walked. "Thank you for agreeing to my strange offer, Pris."

"I never like to see anyone cornered."

"I am fortunate you are my ally."

She laughed and tapped his nose. "I am—if you will be so kind to recall—your fiancée."

He wrinkled his nose in a disgusted expression because he knew that was what she expected from him. What he had expected, too. Instead there was this most peculiar flush of pleasure at her words. He warned himself not to get caught up in their deception.

She rubbed her hands together, once again serious. "Tell me, Neville, what happens later?"

"Later?" He had not expected Priscilla to try to corner him into more of a commitment. That was one of the things he appreciated most about her. She accepted their friendship—and whatever their friendship was becoming—without hounding him about where it might lead.

"Don't look so taken aback." Her laugh was brittle, and he knew she was more shaken than she wished him to know. About the apparent attack on Orysia? Or about pretending to be his betrothed? "I am not seeking a promise to meet me at the altar, but I am asking how you intend to put an end to this betrothal of convenience without a great deal of inconvenience."

"We will think of something."

"That won't disappoint the children?"

He grinned. "They have been less obvious about their matchmaking than when I last saw you."

"They love you, Neville." She dampened her lips. "You know that."

"And I love them." He smoothed her hair back from her face. "I would never do anything to hurt them. You know that."

"I do."

He held up his hands. "Please, Pris. Not in my hearing."

Her laugh this time was more genuine. "I would vow not to do that, but I suspect any vows would distress you just now."

"Go to your rooms, Pris." He kissed her on the forehead and stepped away before he swept her into his arms and kissed her as he wanted to. "Lock the door until I return."

"Where are you going?" All humor vanished from her eyes, and the fear he hated to see there reappeared.

"I need to check something. I will be back quickly. Go to your rooms, and do not open the door unless you know I am on the other side."

"All right." She stroked his right arm. "Be careful, Neville."

"I will be."

"After all, I don't want to have to plan our wedding all by myself." Her laugh was again forced.

Neville winked, but felt no more like doing that than she wished to laugh. Before he could linger and sample more of her kisses, he walked out into the storm. He hunched as the windblown rain barraged him. Mud squished beneath his boots.

He walked past Miss Young's tent. He heard loud voices but did not pause to discover if Lady Stenborough was accusing her husband of infidelity . . . again.

He went to Orysia's wagon. He was not sure what he was hoping to find, but he had to look. As he reached the open door, something snagged on his foot. He picked up a piece of rope. He balanced it in his hands, wrapping it around his fists. It was the right length for a man to hold around Orysia's throat.

Mayhap she had not been concocting a story to get everyone's sympathy. Mayhap someone *had* tried to kill her. He wished he could figure out why. If he did, he might have the answer to the atrocious events of the day. If he did not, he guessed the dawn would bring more death to the Faire.

FOURTEEN

Priscilla knew her hopes for a much better day were about to be dashed when Aunt Cordelia burst into her bedchamber. The thick oak door slammed behind her aunt, and her daughters looked up from where she had been brushing their hair. They were almost ready to go for breakfast before they returned to Stonehall-on-Sea. Only their departure would have persuaded her aunt to rise so early, because Aunt Cordelia preferred Town hours of entertainments long into the night and rising late the next day.

"Priscilla Emberley Flanders, I never thought you would be *this* thoughtless," Aunt Cordelia stated without the courtesy of a "Good morning."

"Excuse me? Do sit down. You look very pale, Aunt Cordelia." She did not give into the appeal of adding her aunt's full name, Cordelia Emberley Smith Gray Dexter, a litany of the husbands she had buried. When Priscilla saw her daughters exchange uneasy glances, she added, "Why don't you go out into the other chamber and sit with your brother while Aunt Cordelia and I talk?"

Again the girls looked at each other; then Leah piped up, "We want to stay, Mama."

"See?" Aunt Cordelia flung a hand in their direction, her face now as red as the coverlet on the tester bed. "Another example of their poor upbringing! They do not even heed a request from their own mother."

"Nonsense." Priscilla sat on the chaise longue.

Her daughters shifted so they flanked her. She wanted to thank them for their attempt to protect her from her aunt, who could be a virago when provoked, and it was clear something had aggravated Aunt Cordelia this morning.

"I enjoy my children's company," she continued, "and I am pleased they enjoy mine."

"And we want to hear why you are angry with Mama." Leah clapped a hand over her mouth as her eyes widened.

"That is enough," Priscilla said before her aunt could explode. "Aunt Cordelia, do come and sit with us."

Aunt Cordelia folded her arms in front of her still-magnificent figure. "I do not believe I can sit when I am so infuriated at you."

"At me? Why?"

"Because you have accepted an offer from *that man.*"

Daphne squealed and jumped to her feet. "Mama, are you going to marry Uncle Neville?"

Leah flung her arms around Priscilla and squeezed her until Priscilla had to peel away her arms before she was choked. Kissing her mother on the cheek, Leah ran to the door and threw it open.

Priscilla came to her feet, but she could not halt her daughter from yelling, "Isaac, Mama and Uncle Neville are getting married!"

Bounding into the room, Isaac shouted in excitement as he grasped his sisters' hands and danced in a circle.

One glance at her aunt, who was wearing that all-too-familiar disapproving frown, was enough for Priscilla to quiet her children. They became abruptly silent and looked at their great-aunt. This time when Priscilla suggested they wait in the outer chamber, all three went without a word. Each of them offered her an encouraging smile.

Closing the door behind them, Priscilla faced her aunt. She had known this was going to happen when she came to Neville's aid last night, but she had thought she might be able to sneak out with the children to enjoy breakfast before this confrontation.

"Tell me what is in the air is not true," Aunt Cordelia said, her eyes narrowed and sparking.

"I wish I could tell you what you want to hear, but I will never lie to you. Neville asked me to accept his offer of a betrothal, and I did."

"Your husband must be ready to push his way out of his barely cold grave to beg you to have some sense."

Priscilla scowled. If her aunt thought she would get her way by reminding Priscilla of how Lazarus had died less than two years before, she was mistaken. Sadly mistaken. Raising her chin, she said, "I will ask you to recall, Aunt Cordelia, the lasting and deep friendship between my husband and Neville."

"Simply because you married a beef-head once is no reason to make the same error again." Her eyes widened. "Same? Marrying *that man* would be a hundredfold worse. I cannot imagine how you could make the same mistake twice."

"I will ask you not to insult either Lazarus or Neville." She bit back her anger. Bellowing like two fishmongers would solve nothing. "If you took the time to get to know Neville, really get to know him—"

"I don't need to be well acquainted with a thief to know I will not invite him into my house. Yet you want to invite *that man,* who has been a thief and heavens knows what else, into our *family!* Do that, Priscilla, and you will be very sorry."

"Aunt Cordelia, please do not resort to threats."

Her aunt walked toward her and wagged a finger directly in front of Priscilla's nose. "'Tis no threat, Priscilla. 'Tis a fact that there are many in our family who are greatly alarmed by your lack of judgment in choosing where you give your heart."

"Choose? When has anyone ever had a choice about where one's heart goes?" She laughed. Instantly she regretted it, because her aunt's expression grew even more furious.

"Put an end to this betrothal posthaste."

"Or?"

Aunt Cordelia replied in her haughtiest tones, "I shall have the family's support in removing you from any influence over your children." She stamped out of the room, once more sending the door crashing in her wake.

Priscilla bit her lip as she wove her trembling fingers together. Her aunt meant what she said. As the family's matriarch, she would be able to sway many to her opinion. Priscilla had won the battle over where Isaac would attend school, but so many times her aunt had complained that Priscilla had no idea of how to raise an earl properly. Never had Aunt Cordelia threatened to take her daughters away as well.

Dropping to the chaise longue, she wondered how

something that had seemed like a favor for a very dear friend had become such a muddle. She must find Neville and speak with him. It should be simple to explain how they must put an end to this charade.

Yet it was not. She ran a finger along the length of the fourth finger on her left hand and over her wedding ring. The simple gold band that Lazarus had given her when they pledged to love each other until death parted them glistened in the light coming past the green draperies. She had planned to wear it until, by some happenstance, a man came into her life, bringing a new love with him.

Slowly she slipped the ring off her finger and onto one of the hair ribbons she had intended to use in Leah's hair. She tied the ribbon around her neck, making sure it was tucked out of sight beneath her bodice.

Only then did she walk to the door. She would find Neville and explain they must put an end to this hoax, but she would have to guard every word she spoke. She could not let him guess she wanted him to persuade her to stand up to this appalling threat from her aunt . . . because they were making their betrothal a real one.

Where had *that* thought come from? She was unsure, but she needed to suppress it. Matters were too dire to allow herself such fancies, especially where Neville Hathaway was involved.

Constable Forshaw stood in the shadows by the castle and stared around the midway. If he had not known better, he would have thought everything was as merry as the Faire actors pretended.

He was stumped. There was no other word for it.

Other crimes had left tantalizing clues, but with this one there seemed to be nothing but disconnected events. A man shot by a crossbow and killed; another wounded. Two men killed in what might have been a fight or a murder and a suicide. Another man slashed by a knife when a fight occurred. A woman almost strangled in her own wagon. What did they have in common?

He drew out his pipe and lit it from a nearby brand someone had stuck into the ground. Raising a cloud of smoke sometimes helped to clear his mind. He puffed, but no inspiration burst into his brain.

When he saw a familiar form swathed in pink, he strode on an intersecting path. Lady Priscilla could be exasperating, but her agile mind might be able to offer the very clue he was searching for.

Priscilla paused when she heard Constable Forshaw speak her name. Her children did the same until she told them to go to the area where breakfast was being served to the guests who had risen early. She asked them to wait for her before they ate and smiled when her son grimaced. Isaac was always hungry.

"Good morning," Priscilla said when Constable Forshaw stopped next to her. She wondered if he had slept. If he had, it had been in his clothes, by the number of wrinkles in his coat. The gray arcs under his eyes were darker than they had been before.

He puffed on his pipe. "I hope it will be a good one."

"I assume then that nothing further is amiss." She wafted the smoke away from her face.

"That is a good assumption."

"That is good."

When he regarded her with obvious curiosity, she knew she must sound silly repeating his words back to him. She had tried to focus on their conversation, but her thoughts were on what she would say to Neville and how she would say it. Bother! She wished she had never stepped forward to announce their betrothal last night. If Neville's offer had not unsettled her so much, she would have realized the mistake such a charade would be.

"Yes, it is good." He sounded as unconvinced and ill at ease as she was.

Priscilla clasped her hands. "You do not sound as if things are good."

"You are right. Nothing can be good when a murderer walks about free to kill again, and I have no idea where to seek him. I don't even know where to begin."

"Constable Forshaw," she said as she straightened her shoulders, "an excellent place to begin would be to insist Lord Stenborough put an end to the Faire."

"I would gladly do that."

"But . . . ?"

"As I have told you, he refuses to listen, and I do not yet have a legal reason to insist he does."

"Yet?"

"Do not pounce on every word I say, my lady."

Priscilla relented. He was right. She was acting as skittish as Miss Young when Lady Stenborough was nearby. "Forgive me, Constable. I am out of sorts this morning."

"Something I believe I am as well. Lady Priscilla, I—"

"Lady Priscilla! Lady Priscilla! Lady Priscilla!"

Priscilla whirled. Orysia rushed toward them.

Halting the young woman, Priscilla asked, "Why are you running so fast on this warm morning?"

"It is horrible. Just horrible!"

"What is horrible?" asked a deep voice. Not Constable Forshaw's, but—

"Sir Neville!" cried Orysia, for once not putting the snide emphasis on his title. "Thank heavens you are here."

"What is it?" He glanced at Priscilla.

She wanted to take his arm and draw him aside where they could speak about the muddle their feigned betrothal had created. She watched Orysia grasp on to his sleeve.

"Breakfast! Something is wrong with breakfast. Everyone is ill."

"Everyone?" asked Priscilla.

"Everyone," Orysia choked. "They have been poisoned! They are going to die."

If Orysia said more, Priscilla did not hear it. She pushed past her and followed as Neville and Constable Forshaw raced toward the area where breakfast was being served. Gathering up her skirt to an unseemly height, she tried to catch up. She bounced off one person, then another who was trying to flee. Fearful voices struck her ears, and groans came from where sick people were lying in rows like graves in a churchyard. She flinched at that thought.

While she searched for her children among the eddies of people, she saw Neville talking to Orysia. The fortune-teller was waving her hands frantically. Then Priscilla saw Daphne coming toward her, holding Leah by one hand and Isaac by the other.

She hugged them. "Are you all right?"

"Yes," Daphne said.

"Did you eat anything?"

"No," said Daphne and Leah at the same time.

Isaac put his hand on his stomach. "I did. Am I going to be sick, too?"

Taking his hand, she went to where Neville was helping a man lie down before he collapsed. "Neville, Isaac ate some of the food."

He assisted the groaning man to the ground, then asked, "Isaac, what did you eat?"

"Not much." He stared down at his feet.

"What exactly?"

"Not much, just some muffins with butter and jam. Oh, I had an egg and some fried mushrooms and—"

"Not much?" asked Neville, arching an eyebrow.

"Not much for him." Priscilla tried to smile, but it was impossible.

Isaac put his hand on his stomach again. "I don't feel very good."

"It may be his imagination," Priscilla said as Isaac dropped onto a bench.

"I hope you are right." He paused as two women began to retch. Lifting Isaac carefully so he did not unduly jostle the boy, he said, "I think we should take him to your rooms."

She nodded and put an arm around her daughters' shoulders. As she started toward the manor house, someone grasped her skirt.

"Lady Stenborough!" she gasped. She motioned for the girls to hurry after Neville, then bent down.

The viscountess was a strange shade of gray as she clutched her stomach. She shuddered and moaned. Opening one eye, she whispered, "Lady Priscilla?"

"Where do you hurt?"

"My stomach. First it felt as if someone were pounding a fist into it over and over. Now it feels as if it is being wrung out by hard fingers."

Wishing she could offer more than sympathy, Priscilla said, "Lie still. It might help."

"Nothing helps." She groaned, her knees rising toward her belly.

"I am sure the doctor has been sent for. If not, we will dispatch him as soon as we get back to the house."

Lady Stenborough's fingers grasped her wrist. "How long?"

"As soon as I can." She slipped her hand past the viscountess's weak fingers. "I am going now."

Rising, Priscilla walked toward the house. She looked back when she heard a shriek of pain. A man doubled over before falling to his knees. So many people ill.

Not an illness, she realized as servants rushed to help. Orysia had spoken of poison. She hoped that the fortune-teller had been wrong and that this was caused by food gone bad.

She took a step and bumped into someone. She started to apologize as she stepped around him so she could get to her son, but froze as heavy hands clamped on to her shoulders.

"Lord Stenborough, what—"

"I have to speak with you."

Priscilla shrugged his hands off her shoulders and gave him a frown that she hoped would show he would be wise not be so forward again. "I must tend to my son. He ate some of the tainted food."

The viscount kept her from edging around him. "Please, Lady Priscilla. It is important."

"So is my son!"

"And you will let other people be endangered because of it?"

"Of course not." Bother! She did not want to linger and listen to him bemoan the shambles of his birthday celebration. "Lord Stenborough, what do you expect me to do?"

"Help me discover why this happened."

"I know very little about Stenborough Park and the Faire."

"But you are observant." His lips stretched into a tight smile. "I have seen that. Constable Forshaw has mentioned that."

"You are kind, but no amount of compliments will get your questions answered when I have nothing to tell you. I was not there when Duncan was wounded or when Mr. Harmsworth was killed—"

"When he killed himself."

"*Was* killed. When he *was* killed, I was going back to the manor house with Neville."

"I know." His eyes narrowed. "How did he act?"

"He? Neville? I don't understand what you mean. He acted like Neville." The memory of Neville's touch and his eager invitation to find time away from the Faire flooded her with warmth. She would not share that with the viscount.

"Did he act nervous?"

"No."

"Was he in a hurry to get to the feast yesterday?"

"No."

"Then he was dawdling?"

"No, although we took a circuitous route to get around the crowd looking for seats at the tables."

Lord Stenborough demanded, "Haven't you realized that he did not want you there before the quarrels were fired?"

Priscilla swallowed roughly. Lord Stenborough suspected Neville was involved in these attacks. That Neville Hathaway might have a hand in murder was ludicrous. So why was Lord Stenborough accusing him? Did he have facts she did not? Not that they would prove Neville was guilty of the deaths, but they might give her a clue to expose the true murderer.

"What makes you think that?" she asked with caution.

"I—I—I really should not say."

"Then I ask you to excuse me so that I may go to my son."

As she walked past him, he seized her arm. She yelped more in shock than pain. She peeled his fingers off her arm, slapping away his hand when he reached for her again.

"Lady Priscilla," he insisted, "you have to listen to me, for your own safety."

"You have said nothing worth listening to. I would trust Neville with my life and the lives of my children."

His tongue scraped along his lips. "I hope you do not come to rue that, my lady."

"As I hope you do not rue Neville discovering you are defaming him in this manner."

She walked away. It was about time to get to the bottom of this . . . as soon as she knew Isaac would be all right.

"He is sleeping." Priscilla closed the bedroom door. As she crossed the outer chamber, she wiped her hands on the apron she had borrowed from a maid. "Where are Daphne and Leah?"

"With your aunt." Neville handed her a cup, and she drew in the succulent aroma of coffee. "She seems a bit more distressed with me than is customary. Has she, by chance, heard—?"

"Sit down. There are several things we need to talk about."

"That sounds serious."

"Neville, don't jest with me now."

His smile faded, and he motioned for her to sit on the settee. "Are you hungry, Pris? I went down to the kitchen and brought up some food that I cooked myself."

"You cooked? I had no idea you had such skills."

"I did not always have servants to tend to those things for me." He gave her a gentle smile as he picked up a tray with some fresh fruit and sliced vegetables on it and offered it to her.

She shook her head. "After seeing what poor Isaac has suffered, I am not sure I ever want to eat again. Why don't you sit?"

"Thanks, Pris," he said as he sat. Fatigue dimmed his eyes and lined his cheeks which were shadowed with dark whiskers.

"You look horrible."

"Mayhap because I feel horrible." He brushed at his stained shirt. "I would like to take a bath for about two or three hours."

"First we must talk."

"'Tis more than your aunt's reaction to our supposed betrothal that is upsetting you. Is it more than Isaac being ill?"

"Lord Stenborough believes you committed the murders!" Priscilla clamped her lips closed. "I am sorry, Neville. I should not have spoken so abruptly. I am afraid I am more all on end than I had believed I was."

"I see." He stirred his coffee, then took a sip. Setting himself on his feet, he walked to the window that offered a view of the Faire. He put the cup on the sill and leaned his right hand on the window's wide frame.

She waited for him to say something more, but he remained silent. Slowly she stood. She went to stand behind him, putting her hand against his back.

"Pay him no mind, Neville. Why do you care what he believes when it is not true?"

"I don't care what he thinks."

"Constable Forshaw knows you have an alibi for every attack. Me."

"Nor do I care what Forshaw thinks."

"Then what is bothering you?"

He continued to look out the window, his fingers closing into a fist against it. "Myself."

"Pardon me?"

Facing her, he took her left hand in his. His eyes widened when he touched her fourth finger. "You took off your wedding ring, Pris?"

"Yes."

"As part of our charade?"

"I thought it would be unlikely that a betrothed woman would wear the ring from her first marriage." She drew out the ribbon she had tied around her neck. Putting her hand on the ring that hung over her heart, she whispered, "I put it here so I would not lose it."

"You will never lose what you and Lazarus had."

She smiled, so glad he understood what she found impossible to put into words. "I know."

"Tell me what Lady Cordelia said, Pris."

Closing her eyes, she leaned her head on his unhurt shoulder. "She has threatened to take the children from me now that I have proven I am so witless as to accept your proposal."

He ground out a word through his clenched teeth, a word Priscilla would have scolded Isaac for saying. "You know she is trying to intimidate you."

"She is doing a fine job." She raised her eyes to meet his furious gaze. "Don't say what you are about to say. This is not like it was when she tried to insist on deciding which school Isaac would attend or which friends Daphne should have. I believe this time she is willing to carry out her threats."

"Pris, I am sorry. What I thought would help both of us has taken a dark turn." He glanced about the room. "Like everything else at this accursed estate." Holding her face in his hands, he said, "It may be one of the shortest betrothals ever, but it is clear we must bring it to an end."

"I will tell Aunt Cordelia."

"She would prefer a public ending to it. A very loud and unequivocal ending. I do recall a scene from one play I did where the female lead almost knocked my teeth from my head during such a scene. I would request you do not give your aunt that much satisfaction."

Priscilla chuckled. "You are a devil, Neville Hathaway."

"So I have been told many times."

"By whom?"

"You."

She welcomed his lips on hers as her arms slid up his back, slipping beneath his coat. Even while she relished his eager kiss, she took care not to brush the bandaging near his shoulder. Nothing should interrupt this perfect moment. She could not keep from imagining him holding her pressed to his naked chest. Every inch of her begged to tell him that she cared nothing about her aunt's threats, that she wanted their silly, fake betrothal to continue until it had a chance of becoming a genuine one.

Her breath puffed out in a soft moan when he

trailed kisses along her neck. Holding him close with one hand, she combed the fingers of the other through his dark hair. His whiskers scoured her skin, and the very maleness of it thrilled her. She whispered his name just before he claimed her mouth anew.

"Is anyone within? I—oh, I am sorry."

As Neville released her, Priscilla saw a red-faced Constable Forshaw in the doorway.

"I knocked," the constable said, rocking from one foot to the other as Isaac did when he had done something wrong.

Neville laced his fingers through hers as he asked, "What do you need, Constable?"

"Do you know where Lord Stenborough is?"

Neville shrugged, then gingerly touched his bandaged shoulder. "Probably at the Faire."

"He is not there."

"Then I would suggest you ask his majordomo or housekeeper where he might be."

Priscilla said, "Wait here." She rang a bell but was not surprised when no one came to answer it. The servants must be hiding, afraid to do or say anything after the sickness at breakfast.

"I will go and find someone," Constable Forshaw said. "That will allow you to finish your—your—your conversation."

Heat scored Priscilla's face, and she hoped it was not as crimson as the constable's. "Thank you."

"Wait, Constable." Neville went toward him. "Why do you need Stenborough now?"

"I need to talk to him about what has happened."

"Why? He seems to believe I had a hand in all of it."

"Neville!" Had he lost his mind?

He smiled at her. "Pris, if I don't tell him, Stenborough is sure to feed him the nonsense he tried to get you to swallow."

Constable Forshaw looked from Neville to her. "Sir Neville, is this one of your jokes?"

Neville used a tone colder than she had ever heard from him. "I find nothing about murder, attempted murder, and today's sickness amusing. It is barbaric. Suggesting that I had something to do with it is as unconscionable as letting this Faire continue."

"It will not be continuing. I am putting an end to the Faire. That is why I am seeking Lord Stenborough. He must heed good sense *now.*"

Neville laughed grimly. "And do you think that stopping the rest of the day's entertainments is really going to halt whoever is behind this, Constable Forshaw? Someone is after something, and that person will not stop until he gets what he wants, or all of us are dead. Or both."

FIFTEEN

The knock at the door startled Priscilla. She rose from where she had been watching her son sleep. Who could it be? Neville had gone with Constable Forshaw to look for Lord Stenborough. She doubted the constable would return alone.

Rising from her chair, she went to the bedchamber's door. She glanced back to see her son still asleep on the simple bed that denoted this room was for a guest's personal servants.

A maid waited on the other side of the door. She dipped in a quick curtsy as she said, "M'lady, Mr. McAndrews has requested that you and Sir Neville come to his room."

"You must look for Sir Neville. I need to stay with my son."

"Mr. McAndrews told me to tell you that he wants to take you away from Lord Emberson's bedside for only a few minutes. I will sit with him, if you please, m'lady." The brown-haired maid lowered her eyes. "I have some experience in the stillroom, so I know how to look for signs of a turn for the worse."

Priscilla nodded. That Duncan knew Isaac had been ill suggested Neville's friend was feeling well enough to heed the gossip flitting about the manor house. And what he wished to talk to her and Neville about must be very important.

"Send for me immediately if there is any change, especially if he wakes." She started for the hallway door, then paused. "Is someone else seeking Sir Neville to give him the message?"

"Yes, m'lady."

"If there is any change, send for me posthaste."

"Yes, m'lady."

Even with that assurance, Priscilla had to force her feet to carry her out of the room. Isaac was deeply asleep after vomiting everything he had in his stomach. She would be back soon. Her steps faltered. If Aunt Cordelia returned before Priscilla did, there would be perdition to pay.

That thought was enough to spur her along the passages until she reached the one where Duncan's room was. She took a deep breath, for Dr. Dommel might be within.

A light rap brought a command in Duncan's brogue to enter. She opened the door cautiously, not wishing to intrude into an embarrassing situation. When she saw he was sitting up in bed, the covers pulled over his chest, she stepped in. She started to leave the door ajar so there would be no question of impropriety. Then, realizing someone might eavesdrop, she closed the door before crossing the room.

"My lady." Duncan gave her a feeble smile. "Pardon me for not standing."

She drew a chair beside the bed and sat. "There."

"Thank you." He looked past her. "Where is Neville?"

"A servant is trying to find him."

"The doctor will be returning soon. He went out to light up a cheroot, and that was quite some time ago."

Priscilla clenched her hands. People were sick throughout the grounds of Stenborough Park, and Dr. Dommel was enjoying his cigar. Reminding herself that she should not be thinking about the doctor when Duncan had something important to share, she asked, "Will you tell me now why you sent for us so I may inform Neville as soon as I see him?"

"Yes. I need to speak with someone, or I daresay I shall burst."

"Have you remembered something about when you were wounded?"

He lowered his voice to a whisper, his gaze focused on the door. "Just before I was hit, I saw a glint of gold at the far end of the banquet area."

"By the briars?"

"Yes. I thought the glint was on the other side of the briars, but there is a wall behind them. It had to have been *in* the briars."

"Gold? What kind? Like jewelry?"

He shook his head. "More like the piping on a hat. The gold was fabric, not metal."

"Are you sure it was a hat? Could it have been on a shoulder or a waistcoat?"

"Not unless the person was very tall. I suspect it was part of a costume worn by one of the actors."

She tapped her chin as she mused, "I wonder who wears a hat that color."

"You should speak with the person in charge of the troupe's costumes."

"Duncan, what a brilliant suggestion!"

"I have long believed I was a genius. My only problem has been persuading others to believe the same."

She laughed. "I—"

The door opened, and Dr. Dommel entered. "Mr. McAndrews, you need to rest. Oh, Lady Priscilla, I did not see you here." His mouth straightened. "I had thought you would be with your fiancé."

"Fiancé?" asked Duncan, sitting straighter.

"Don't you know?" asked Dr. Dommel, his tone snide. "Lady Priscilla and Sir Neville have announced their intentions to wed."

Duncan gave a hearty laugh. "I warned him to watch himself around you. So the fox has finally been run to earth, has he? When will the nuptials be?"

"We have not discussed that yet." She wished Neville had never broached the idea of a fake betrothal. "I shall bid you gentlemen a good day, if you will excuse me. I suspect Dr. Dommel wishes you to rest, Duncan."

"I am too old for a nap," he protested.

"I am going to go . . ." She glanced at the doctor and back at Duncan. "I will find out that answer for you."

"Be careful," he said to her back.

She turned. Anxiety lengthened his face. She gave him a tense smile.

"Be careful?" Dr. Dommel asked sharply.

"Not to eat anything without knowing how it was prepared," she replied. She hurried out of the room. As she went along the corridor, she tried to ignore the shiver of premonition coursing through her like a cold river. She was not superstitious, but too much had happened at the Faire in the past day and a half for her not to wonder what trouble asking these questions might bring.

The Faire was as deserted as if the Black Death had swept down upon it. Priscilla did not see anyone among the tents. She squinted into the bright midday sun. No, she was not mistaken. More than half of the tents had vanished. She wished they could have been part of the exodus, but traveling before Isaac was well was out of the question. On the morrow, if he recovered quickly, they could return to Stonehall-on-Sea.

A quick stop at her rooms had revealed her son still slept, his face regaining its normal color. The maid was willing to sit with him for the short time longer.

Priscilla glanced at the sun and frowned. The modiste with their costumes for the masquerade tonight was supposed to arrive this afternoon. Priscilla hoped the seamstress would not arrive until after she had had a chance to eat something.

She walked toward the wagons where the actors lived. No more of them had left, so she guessed they were willing to stay in hopes of getting paid. The occasional voice—hushed and furtive—came from the tents set up in front of the castle. She paused by Orysia's, but heard nothing within. Mayhap it was just as well. She did not trust the fortune-teller not to twist anything that happened to her advantage.

She saw a lad trying to juggle. He was chasing more balls across the ground than he was catching. Greeting him, she asked, "Which wagon belongs to Mr. Bennett?"

He pointed to one painted a simple white. "That one, m'lady, but 'e's not there."

"Where is he?"

"Went to talk to Milord Stenborough, I suspect."

She did not want to be drawn into another conversation with Lord Stenborough, so she asked, "Can you tell me which wagon holds your costumes?"

Giving her a puzzled look, he told her to go to the

wagon that had no windows and was painted a faded orange. It was set off from the others in a position that would make it convenient for costume changes.

She thanked him. If Mr. Bennett was dismayed at her going into the costume wagon without his permission, she would apologize and explain.

As she wove a path through the wagons, Priscilla could not get one question out of her mind. Who? Who was trying to kill and hurt people? Each time some facet of the Faire had been involved. Was the murderer creative or simply using the tools at hand?

The smells of food cooking and smoke drifted between the wagons. Her stomach gurgled, and she recalled that she had skipped breakfast. As soon as she returned to her rooms, she would sample Neville's tray of vegetables.

When she reached the costume wagon, the door was open. She climbed the few steps. Smoke tickled her nose, and she wondered who was burning green wood.

Several trucks were open. Costumes and props were scattered about the floor. Were they being taken out or being packed away so the troupe could leave? Mayhap Mr. Bennett had gone to obtain the troupe's fee from the viscount.

She took a step inside and recoiled from the heat building up in it. The day was overly warm for Michaelmas Day, but she had not expected the interior to be as hot as this. She started to leave, then saw a flash of gold. Kneeling, she stabbed her hand into a trunk. She pulled out a green wool hat with gilt trim on its narrow brim. Her eyes widened as she saw a broken purple feather stuck into the band.

The archer must have been wearing this. At last something concrete they could use as a clue.

Smoke tickled her nose, and she sneezed.

Smoke?

She looked down and saw gray, misty fingers of smoke oozing up through the spaces between the floorboards. There must be a fire beneath the wagon. She whirled, and the door slammed shut in her face.

"No!" she cried. "Don't shut it. I am in here!"

Everything was lost in darkness. Everything but the smoke. She could not hear the crackle of flames, but she must escape before the wagon caught fire.

Shoving the hat into her bodice so she would not lose it, she lurched toward the door and fell over some shoes. Blood trickled down her scraped knee. She fought to breathe. She had to stand and put as much distance as possible between her and the smoke. Pushing herself up, she groped for the door. She shoved against it, but the door did not open. She tried again. The door did not budge. She pounded on it.

"I am in here! Let me out!" She pounded again.

Relief filled her when a fist on the other side echoed the rhythm of her knocking. Why wasn't the door opening?

"Let me out!" She hit the door with both fists.

The other fist answered twice.

"Now!" She thumped it again.

The fist banged once.

"Get—me—out!" She punctuated each word with another blow to the door.

Silence.

Horror clamped on her throat. Who knew she was here? Duncan and the boy who had given her directions . . . and whoever had locked her in. Duncan would not be able to tell anyone until someone gave him a look-in. Neville! They had been searching for Neville to send him to Duncan's room. How long would it take to find Neville? She knew him well enough to know he could avoid being found if he did not want to be.

She banged on the door again, hoping one of the actors would hear her. Choking, she leaned her head against the door. This wagon might be too far from the others for anyone to hear her, and the Faire was deserted. Hadn't she been pleased about that a few minutes ago?

Wiping sweat from her nape, she waved her hand in front of her face. The smoke was thickening. She struggled to breathe and listened for the sound of flames. She was grateful for every second it did not come.

Time passed. At least, she thought it did. The smoke clogged her brain, making thinking as hard as breathing. Strange thoughts paraded through her head. She thought she heard laughter, but no one answered her call for help. Mayhap it had been her imagination. Mayhap not.

As the smoke became thicker and thicker, she tried not to gasp for breath. That took too much air. Air? There was not any left. She pressed closer to the door, hoping it would open an inch to let in more air. Any breath, just one more breath, just one more . . . And then all thought vanished.

Priscilla opened one eye cautiously. Dazzling light pierced it. She closed it, hoping all of heaven was not illuminated with such brilliant lights.

"Open your eyes. Show me you are awake."

Neville! She wanted to speak his name, but only a scratchy croak came out.

"Pris, drink this." An arm under her shoulders tilted her up as a cup was held to her lips.

She gulped it greedily. It was cool and fresh and clean.

"Slow down," he ordered, drawing the cup away.

"More. Please, Neville." Her voice still did not sound like her own.

"If you will drink it slowly."

She nodded and sipped. When the water was gone, he refilled the cup and held it to her lips again. His muttered curse warned that he had strained his shoulder.

"I can drink on my own," she murmured, her voice not as raw when she whispered.

"Are you certain?"

"Yes."

He put the cup in her right hand and drew her left fingers around it, too. She knew he had been wise because when he released the cup, she almost dropped it. Balancing it against one drawn-up knee, she sipped and leaned back against pillows set against the arm of the headboard.

Headboard? In amazement, she realized she was lying on her bed in the manor house. How had she gotten here? Her last memory was of smoke in the wagon.

"What in perdition were you doing in a wagon about to catch on fire?" Neville demanded.

"It caught fire?"

"No, it was put out in time. If a lad had not come running to let me know you were in there, we might not have gotten you out in time. When we got there,

Orysia was calling for help to extinguish the fire. She was covered with almost as much soot as you."

"Whoever shut the door planned to add me to the list of murder victims. Thank heavens you broke through the door and—"

"No, there was no need. It was not locked."

"What? That cannot be. I could not open it."

His brows rose. "Be that as it may, it was not locked when we got there. Did you by chance see who closed the door?"

Priscilla sighed. "That would have been too easy."

"So we have no more idea who is behind this than before. What were you doing in there?"

"Looking for . . ." She reached into her bodice. "It is gone!"

"Your wedding ring?"

She smiled as she raised her hand and stroked his cheek, which still was in need of a shave and was streaked with ash. "No, that is not lost. Thank you for caring, Neville."

"I care about anything that is important to you." His smile was swift, but it disappeared as he asked, "What is gone?"

"Duncan remembered seeing some gilt decoration on what he thought must be a hat. I went to see if I could find something like that, and I did. A green hat with gold trim."

"Unique gold trim?"

"I wish I could say it was, but I have seen its like on many gowns. What was unique was a broken purple feather."

His eyes widened. "Indeed."

She leaned toward him, then halted with a moan. She cradled her head in her hands. She had not had such a fearsome headache since . . . She had *never* had such a fearsome headache.

"You put the hat within your bodice?" he asked, his voice sounding as strangled as hers.

"Yes." Her head jerked up. She ignored the pain as she gasped, "Someone must have come in and taken it."

"And then left you there to die."

"Who would do such a horrible thing?" She shuddered. "No, you don't need to answer. The answer is obvious. The person who has been killing Lord Stenborough's guests." She swung her legs over the side of the bed. "How is Isaac? Mayhap we should leave now."

"He is acting as if he had never been ill. The boy was foraging for something to eat when I last spoke with him. He was less worried about his stomach than if he would be able to see the dungeon he is certain Stenborough has hidden in his cellars."

She smiled. "I did promise I would speak with Lord Stenborough about a tour of the cellars so Isaac would see for himself the dangers of listening to gossip."

"As the boy is hale, if you wish, we can go back to Stonehall-on-Sea straightaway."

"We? You would leave before you found out who shot your friend?"

"Not happily, but I will."

She shook her head, then put her hand to her temple. She had to be more cautious. "What time is it?"

"Midafternoon."

"So late?"

"Yes. You have been keeping the *modiste* waiting more than an hour."

She started to ask which *modiste*, then recalled the one Neville had hired to make costumes for them to wear to the masquerade tonight. Pushing herself off the bed and to her feet, she grasped Neville as he put his arm around her waist.

"Take care," he said. "You breathed in a great quantity of smoke. You should sit while I get you some tea to soothe your stomach."

She leaned back on the chaise longue, closing her eyes again. He placed a damp cloth gently on her forehead and lightly massaged her temples. Relaxing against the cushions, she let his fingers blunt the honed pain.

"Leaving just now," she said, "does not seem like the wisest course. By the time we have everything ready to go, it will be close to dark. Don't suggest we leave the servants behind to handle the packing. I will not leave them here to be a madman's prey."

"I assumed you would say that."

She opened one eye to see his smile. "So you were able to agree with me without worrying about actually having to leave."

"Yes."

She laughed. Neville's honesty had never seemed more precious than now.

The door opened, and her children peeked in. Calling to them, she held out her arms. She hugged them and laughed when Isaac told her that she stank like a chimney sweep. Her own nose was so clogged she doubted she could smell anything, but the blinding pain was gone.

Neville let them prattle for a few minutes about the costume that had been delivered for her, then herded them out with the promise that they could return and talk with her before the masquerade ball in the pavilion by the sea. It was said to be far grander than the small one used for the tournament.

"Pavilion?" she asked, astonished. "The masquerade is not here in the manor house?"

"Didn't I mention that Stenborough has set up a make-believe great hall?"

"No, you did *not* mention it. What else have you failed to mention, Neville?"

"Don't wear that expression you use when you are about to scold Isaac. It will not work with me." He became abruptly serious. "I have not kept anything else from you, Pris. I thought I had told you. Egad, I just realized that, as we are breaking off our betrothal before the masquerade, I shall be escorting Miss Young while you go with Dommel."

She came to her feet. "I am sorry, Neville."

"You have no reason to apologize. I was the one who came up with what seemed an inspired idea at the time. I never considered Lady Cordelia's reaction. Then"—he walked to the closed door—"or now."

Priscilla's face grew as warm as it had in the wagon. Even a friendship of so many years and the guise of a betrothal would not grant Neville the privilege of remaining in her bedchamber after she was up and about.

"Pris, you are blushing." He chuckled. "That is rather charming."

"No more teasing. You must take your leave right away. If my aunt—" She began to smile as he chuckled. Trust Neville to figure out a way to watch over her and give them the perfect excuse to end their betrothal at the same time.

Priscilla turned away as tears swarmed into her

eyes. She did not want their fabricated betrothal to be over so soon, although she had known it would have to be as soon as he took his leave of Stonehall-on-Sea. She wanted—she wanted Neville Hathaway as part of every day, not just the times when their lives happened to intersect, often after months apart. But that was not what Neville would want, and she would be foolish to expect it from him. If he were the kind of person to be eager for such an ordinary life, he might no longer be her dear Neville.

"Pris?" he asked, coming to stand behind her. His fingers on her shoulders were a gentle caress. "If you do not feel well enough to make a scene, we can simply explain to your aunt that we made a mistake."

"No, I intend to give Aunt Cordelia what she wants."

"And what about what you want?" Neville's fingers against her cheek as he brushed soot from it, slowly brought Priscilla to face him. He gazed down into her warm eyes, where a man might spend a lifetime exploring each emotion. "What do *you* want, Pris?"

"I don't know." She appeared as surprised as he was at her answer.

"Pris, you probably don't know either that you are as bothersome to me as your aunt is to you."

"What?"

He kept her from stepping away by folding her hands between his. "You are bothersome because you cause me to say things like if there were ever a woman I decided to wed, it would be you."

She stared up at him, then began to laugh.

"I did not expect you to be amused by such a confession," he said.

"You should when you try so hard to sound noble. It does not suit you, Neville." She laughed again.

"But that was a very fine speech, no matter how unwilling each word was."

He shook his head in amusement. When would he recall that Priscilla seldom reacted as other women did?

She walked to the bed and picked up one of the pillows, steadying herself so she did not knock herself off her feet with the slight motion. Raising the pillow, she said, "I believe it is time to make my aunt very happy."

"Me first." He hooked an arm around her waist and tugged her to him.

The pillow dropped to the floor as he captured her sweet lips. Her breath, swift and unsteady, filled his mouth as he tasted the luscious flavors within hers. Even as he savored holding her close, a small, taunting voice in his head was telling him he was a fool to leave this woman and the pleasure they could share. She quivered against him, and it took every bit of his willpower to release her. He must, because if he did not, he was unsure if he could ever let her go.

"For good luck?" she asked, her breathing ragged.

He guessed whatever he replied was the right response, because she laughed as she bent to pick up the pillow. He put his hand under her elbow to keep her from toppling. As soon as she was steady, he drew back his hand, which yearned to touch her far more intimately.

When Priscilla raised her voice and began to berate him for overstepping the bounds of propriety, he struggled not to chuckle. She was no well-trained actress, but her performance needed to be just good enough to satisfy her aunt. As he fired heated words back at her, he watched her eyes twinkle with amusement and a joy that came to life whenever he pulled her close. If the murderer had succeeded in that attempt to kill her, he would never have seen her eyes sparkle again. He had to keep her from danger. He was not sure how, because she would not stop looking for the murderer.

"Get out!" she screeched, and he fought not to laugh as the pillow struck the door behind him.

"Pris, be sensible." He shouted the words, so they would reach through the thick oak. When she threw a shoe at him, almost grazing his ear, he added more quietly, "Be careful, Pris. I would like to come out of this with no more injuries."

She smiled but picked up the other shoe.

He opened the door, glancing over his shoulder to see if anyone was in direct line. When he saw no one was there, he gave Priscilla the slightest nod, and she flung the shoe. He ducked beneath it, then winced when he heard something crash to the floor and shatter. Another door opened, and he heard Lady Cordelia's footsteps.

Priscilla's eyes widened in dismay, and Neville frowned. The charade must not be ruined now.

"If you are going to be such a virago," he snarled, "then I should be more than grateful that this betrothal is over. I should be shouting my happiness from the top of the tallest tower in Stenborough Park."

"Over?" cried Leah, running past him to her mother. "Mama, aren't you going to marry Uncle Neville?"

"I would not marry him if ordered to do so by the Prince Regent himself." Priscilla bristled with a fury that Neville hoped was never aimed at him for real.

"But, Mama, we love Uncle Neville."

Priscilla stepped around her daughter, and his eyes

followed her as she strode past her aunt, who was watching, openmouthed. Dash it! Priscilla was a spectacular woman! That he had known since her husband first introduced them, but he had to acknowledge that now or he might dissolve into laughter at this performance.

"Get out." She pointed to the door to the hallway. "Get out and do not return. I shall not have my reputation—and my children's—sullied like this."

Isaac jumped up. "What did he do, Mama?"

"Do not ask." She almost faltered, and he knew she was trying to decide how to explain this to her children so they were not further distressed. Why hadn't he considered all this when he had asked her to play this game? Her shoulders grew rigid again as she added, "It was too unspeakable . . . even for him!"

Neville turned his back on her and opened the door, knowing he had to make his exit before he was unable to keep from laughing. "Consider my offer of marriage withdrawn."

"And my acceptance, *Sir* Neville."

He faced her, shocked at how she put the exact mocking emphasis on his title as Orysia did. When she winked at him as he had at her so often when they were bamboozling others, he choked back a laugh. He strode out, glancing back to see Priscilla surrounded by her children. Off to one side stood her aunt, grinning broadly.

One problem—the one with her aunt that he must apologize again to Priscilla and the children for creating—was taken care of. Now to the problem of the murderer. He knew that would not be resolved as easily or as quickly.

SIXTEEN

Priscilla adjusted her costume's sleeve and ran her finger along the gold trim basted onto it. She had asked the modiste if there was any gold lace in her sewing basket, and Mrs. Winters had found this among her supplies. Mrs. Winters had been astonished when Priscilla asked for it to be added to her sleeves and to the shawl she was wearing tonight.

Would anyone react to seeing the trim on her costume? It was not identical to what had been on the hat, but it and the purple feather she wore in her upswept hair were intended to catch a single pair of eyes. Daphne had been uncertain why Priscilla wanted to trade a pearl-trimmed turban for the feather matching Daphne's costume, but she had eagerly agreed.

All three children had costumes fit for Queen Elizabeth's court. Isaac had been unwilling to don his outfit until he saw the velvet-lined cape that accompanied it. After getting a promise from his mother that she would speak to Lord Stenborough about letting him look through the cellars in the hope of finding medieval torture machines, he had handed his great-aunt into the carriage as graciously as a courtier.

It was unfortunate Dr. Dommel was not as courte-

ous. After Aunt Cordelia's litany of compliments
about the doctor, many of which were aimed at de-
nouncing Neville, Priscilla wondered if Dr. Dommel
was so assured of his welcome that he had left
Priscilla waiting on the steps while the other carriages went down the avenue and onto the road
leading toward the sea.

A form slipped out of the fog and skulked toward
the steps. It was Orysia. What was the fortune-teller
doing here? Shouldn't she be at the pavilion to en-
tertain Lord Stenborough's guests?

"Lady Priscilla!" Orysia gasped, showing she was
just as surprised to discover Priscilla here. "I thought
you would have left by now."

"Not yet." She was not going to offer an excuse for
Dr. Dommel's tardiness, especially when she had
none.

The fortune-teller climbed the steps. "That is an
interesting costume. What is it supposed to represent?"

"Sunrise," she answered quickly, for she had
known she must be prepared for this question. If she
had worn the turban she lent to Daphne, it would
have been clear that she was supposed to be a mermaid. The dark green fabric dropping from the
bodice suggested the mermaid's tale and the turban
the treasures of the sea. That image had been ruined
by the trim and the purple feather.

"Oh." Orysia wrapped her arms around herself.
"Not a good night for a gathering in an open pavilion."

"Lord Stenborough must have planned for fog. It
is common here by the sea."

"Mayhap." She eyed Priscilla again. "I should go."

"I am sure you have a very busy evening ahead of you."

The fortune-teller smiled. "Yes, I do. A very busy one." She went into the manor house.

Although she was curious about why Orysia was going inside, Priscilla did not follow. She must not give Dr. Dommel any cause to be vexed at *her* if he happened to arrive while she was trailing Orysia. Then Aunt Cordelia would be in another pelter.

It was almost a half hour later that the rattle of harness and the clatter of wheels announced a carriage was approaching. Was this Dr. Dommel at last? She would have been concerned that he had been delayed at Duncan's bedside if Neville had not sought her out before he went to meet Miss Young. Neville had said Duncan was determined to leave with them in the morning, for he believed himself well enough to travel.

The carriage slowed as it emerged from fog that was as thick as the smoke in the storage wagon. *Don't think of that!* She must not let the residual fear linger and cause her to miss a clue to the identity of the person who had tried to kill her and Duncan.

"Forgive me, my lady," Dr. Dommel gushed as a tiger leaped down to open the door and hand her in. "The claims on a doctor's time can be many."

"I understand," she replied in a tone that made it clear she meant the opposite, "for the claims of a mother's time can be countless as well."

"Yes. Yes." He muttered something as she sat beside him. When the door closed and the carriage began down the avenue, he took her hand and added, "I would be remiss if I did not say I am sorry Hathaway treated you abominably."

"It is over." She withdrew her hand. Being rude

was not her intention, but neither did she wish to give him any encouragement that she would welcome his attentions. Bother! She should have suggested Neville and Miss Young accompany them to the pavilion. Although tongues would have wagged at the sight of her and Neville together as friends after their broken betrothal, it would have made this journey far more comfortable.

Dr. Dommel said nothing. Silence ached in her ears as she strained to hear the music that would announce they were near the pavilion. All she heard was a distant thundering. A storm or another horse? She could not tell, because the fog distorted sounds. Usually she enjoyed silence and the company of her thoughts, but this silence seemed malevolent. She told herself it was because she was ill at ease here with Dr. Dommel, but it was not only that. She had been surrounded by noise the past two days. The music from the Faire and the voices of the guests . . . and screams. She would be relieved to reach Stone-hall-on-Sea on the morrow and be done with Stenborough Park.

The rapid pounding came closer. Dr. Dommel started to speak; then the horses screamed as the coachee shouted. The carriage rocked. She grabbed the windowsill, and Dr. Dommel grasped her arm.

The carriage pitched in the opposite direction, and she cried out. He was going to yank her arm from her shoulder. As she shook off his fingers, the carriage continued to tilt. She slid along the seat and slammed into the doctor, who let out a loud curse.

The wheels bounced off the road, and the back of the carriage struck a tree. It careened into another.

She ducked, holding her hands and her thin shawl over her head. Bark struck her elbow, stinging from her shoulder to her fingertips. When Dr. Dommel swore again, she wondered if he had been hit by other debris.

The door was thrown open. The coachee peered inside, holding up a carriage lantern that blinded Priscilla. "Dr. Dommel? My lady? Are you all right?"

"I am fine," Priscilla replied, shaking sensation back into her fingers. "Dr. Dommel?"

"My beautiful carriage," he moaned, then snarled, "Are you out of your mind, Mattwood? You will never sit in the box again."

"Dr. Dommel, 'tis John. He is on the ground. He is hurt pretty bad."

Grumbling, the doctor climbed out of the carriage. Priscilla saw that it was leaning precariously against a tree.

"Who is John?" Priscilla asked.

"The tiger, my lady." Mattwood offered his hand. "I will be glad to hand you out." Fury glistened in his eyes as he added, "The carriage may no longer be safe."

Priscilla stepped out. "What happened?"

"Can't say for sure, my lady, but someone came out of the fog, riding at us. I would swear it was a knight like the ones at the joust yesterday. Not a very big knight, but neither were the ones who rode yesterday." He shivered. "Do you think it could be the ghost of one of the dead men?"

"No, I don't think that is possible. Are you sure of what you saw?"

"Yes . . . No, my lady." He glanced over his shoulder as his name was called.

"Go and take the light for Dr. Dommel to use."

He ran with the lantern into the fog.

The weak light from the lantern remaining on the

carriage suggested the candle would soon glut itself while it was tipped at a dangerous angle. She sat on the step. When the carriage creaked ominously, she jumped to her feet.

Then she heard the pounding again. Was the rider returning to see what damage had been wrought by a careless ride? She peered in both directions, but the fog again masked the source of the sound.

She heard a screech behind her. She spun to see a horse galloping straight toward her. Its rider wore armor that glistened in the faint light. She noticed that before she saw what the rider held.

A jousting lance!

Priscilla jumped to the side. She struck the carriage and pain exploded along her hip. She forgot it as she looked over her shoulder.

A spurt of dirt warned the horse was turning. She raced to hide. As the horse sped toward her, she tripped on the broken platform where the tiger had been standing. She threw herself behind the carriage. Venomous laughter filled the night. The lance sliced into the carriage. Dropping to the ground, she watched in horror as the sharp lance jabbed into the carriage again and again. If she had sought refuge inside it, she would have been skewered.

The horse's hoofs struck the carriage, sending pieces cascading down on her. She wished she could pull the fog around her in a cloak of invisibility. Creeping back beneath the trees, she watched the rider poke one more time at the carriage. The horse shook its head, the metal decoration on its bridle ringing a knell through the night.

When the rider shouted, a crash from the direction of Stenborough Park's gate sent cold horror through her. Was another rider attacking Dr. Dommel and the others? Her eyes widened as she saw a dark mass speed out of the fog.

A carriage! Its lamps cut through the fog as the horse wheeled to attack. The carriage sped past. Dirt hit her, scouring her face.

"Are you all right, Pris?"

Neville! What was Neville doing here in his open carriage? She had thought he was already at the pavilion. At a shriek, she knew Miss Young was with him. Had he lost all sense?

She shouted to him, but the carriage sped up. Dirt and small stones erupted from behind it. She hid her face. A horse's whinny rang through the night. The rider raced toward the carriage. She screamed a warning.

The lance struck it. Miss Young's cry of horror was muted by an exultant shout of victory from the rider, who turned to watch Neville's carriage strike Dr. Dommel's. With a hand raised in a salute, the rider slapped the horse and sent it into the eddying mist.

As the hoofbeats vanished into the night, Priscilla heard curses from the carriage. She raced toward it and choked when she saw the broken lance impaling the back of the driver's seat.

"Neville? Miss Young?" she called.

She got no answer. Cupping her hands over her mouth, she shouted, "Dr. Dommel, come straightaway! I think two more are hurt."

"We are alive, Pris." When Neville's fingers touched her arm, she flung her own around him. She pressed her face to his chest for a second, then drew back. She saw blood on his forehead and feared he had been grazed by the lance. Drawing off her shawl, she pressed it against his brow.

"Ouch!"

"Hold it there." When he obeyed, she asked, "Have you lost your mind?"

"Not yet." He turned to assist a cowering Miss Young from the carriage. "I wanted to get that blackguard away from you, Pris, so I gave him another target."

"And risked our lives?" demanded Miss Young. "How could you be so foolish?" She gave him no time to answer. Gathering up her long train, she ran toward where Dr. Dommel stood, his mouth agape. "Take me away from this madman."

"Madman?" The doctor scowled. "If you think sending my carriage off the road and injuring my tiger was amusing, Sir Neville—"

"Lady Priscilla *and* Miss Young can attest I am not the person beneath that armor." He pointed along the road. "Whoever it was went back toward Stenborough Park." He sighed. "There will be no catching him now."

Stenborough Park was deserted when Priscilla and Neville arrived on foot, dirty and damp. He had offered his battered carriage to bring the injured tiger back, and Dr. Dommel had insisted Miss Young ride with him in it. She had refused, setting off to the pavilion with the coachee along to safeguard her.

Priscilla was glad Neville had agreed to return to Stenborough Park. She had no interest in appearing at the gathering when the gold trim hung in tatters and her gown clung to her like a cold cloth. The purple feather was broken like the one she had found in the briars. In the thin light of the manor house's entry, she saw that Neville's costume beneath his black cloak was in as poor condition. A torn strip from her ruined shawl was the only bit of color on his face.

"You should rest," she said, although she knew he would not.

"Nonsense. 'Tis nothing more than an attempt to knock some sense into my hard head. I think we should change and attend Stenborough's celebration." He winked, grimaced, and began to walk out the door.

She ran after him and put her hand on his arm. "Where are you going?"

"To change. My things are in my tent."

"The rider may be nearby."

He stroked her face. "Pris, whoever did that knows better than to loiter here."

"I hope you are right. By the way, why were you and Miss Young so late in going to the pavilion?"

"Jealous, Pris?"

"You keep hoping for that, don't you?"

He chuckled. "To own the truth, Miss Young could not decide which costume to wear to make Lord Stenborough jealous so he would confess his eternal love to her. I fear I am too accustomed to your sensible ways, because I almost left without her."

"I am glad you stayed, so you could come to our rescue." She ran her hand along his right arm. "Be careful when going to your tent, please."

"Fine words for a woman who is supposed to be on the outs with me because I broke off our betrothal."

"You will have to pretend to be burdened with me for the rest of the evening."

He took her hand and raised it to his lips. The gentle kiss flooded her with delight and longing for a more fiery one. "Even an actor as skilled as I cannot be convincing in some roles."

She touched his cheek. "I have a great deal of confidence in you, Neville."

"And I have a great deal of longing to kiss your lips instead of your fingers." He drew her close, but before he could kiss her, he wobbled.

Clasping his arms, she said, "Mayhap you should come to my rooms and rest."

"Are you planning to put me to bed and tuck me in, Pris?"

"If I knew it would keep you there instead of going to the pavilion."

"I have a suggestion that would keep me there." His eyes twinkled merrily.

"I wager you do." She kissed his cheek lightly. "It is clear you are more fit than you wish me to believe. Go and change. I will meet you on the steps as soon as I have done the same."

He became as serious as a judge intoning a sentence on a criminal. "Wait in your rooms, Pris. I will come there to get you."

"All right. I will wait there." She hurried along the empty hallway to the stairs leading up toward her rooms. What Neville had not said added speed to her feet. She understood his worry that she might become a target again if she were alone on the steps.

Was he as dissatisfied as she that they would leave on the morrow with no answer to who had carried out these crimes? Although Neville had shared her suspicions about Mr. Harmsworth, that idea had been dashed when Mr. Harmsworth had come to an end and the attacks had not.

She saw something on the floor of the upper corridor. Not something! Lady Stenborough!

She dropped to her knees next to the viscountess. Blood inched across the floor. When she pushed aside an ornate ruby necklace, she found the lady's heartbeat. Lady Stenborough was still alive, but she might not be for long if left where she was.

She stood as a shadow climbed the wall in front of her. Before she could shout to send for Dr. Dommel, pain careened through her skull. Everything disappeared into a fathomless well of agony.

Priscilla did not know whether it was seconds or an hour later when she awoke. Pain throbbed across her head. Beneath her back was something incredibly uncomfortable, and her legs seemed to be paralyzed because she could not move them. When her wrists were pulled over her head, she moaned a protest. Every motion hurt.

She opened her eyes and frowned. Bare gray stone walls and the same stone was overhead. Where was she?

When she tried to lower her hand, she realized it was now bound with rough rope. She tugged on it. What was going on? She tried again to free her hand.

"Do not move." The tip of something hard was pressed to her temple to second the order.

A pistol!

She looked to her right. "Lord Stenborough!" She stared at the dueling pistol he held. He drew it back, but kept it aimed at her as he held up a candle so the light spread across her. She fought to steady her voice. "I don't know what kind of joke this is, but Lady Stenborough needs a doctor's care. She is lying in the hall. She—"

"Will be dead soon, if I am lucky." He smiled.

A trilling laugh filled her ears and added to the pain across her skull. Priscilla shifted to see Orysia Aleksandovicheva binding the ropes around her wrists to something beyond her view. She tried to pull away and frowned when she heard Orysia laugh again. The fortune-teller was wearing Lady Stenborough's ruby necklace.

Priscilla stared at the necklace, realizing the solution to the puzzle was simple. Lord Stenborough had often been with Orysia when others chanced upon them. He had flirted with Miss Young to hide the fact that his real interest was the fortune-teller. No wonder he had been so eager to bring the Faire and his paramour to Stenborough Park.

"You cannot escape, Lady Priscilla," Orysia murmured. "The rack will hold you well."

"Rack?" In horror, she stared around her. Ropes on her wrists and ankles kept her motionless, but she could see what were unquestionably manacles hanging from a wall and . . . She choked in disgust as she realized the iron container with the spikes was an iron maiden. "Where are we? Is this a part of the Faire?"

"No, my lady." Lord Stenborough used the tip of the pistol to tilt her head back. "Your son has been eager to find out the truth in the rumors about Stenborough Park having an antiquated dungeon. Soon he will know the answer."

"My son! Where is my son?"

He shrugged. "With Lady Cordelia, no doubt."

She tried to keep her voice calm, warning herself not to panic needlessly. "Your joke has gone on long enough. Let me go."

"I do not think so, Lady Priscilla." Lord Stenborough smiled as he nodded.

It was her only warning before agony seared her as the ropes creaked, pulling on the ropes on her arms and ankles. She bit her lip. She would not scream. She could not give them that pleasure.

Lord Stenborough gestured toward the exit. "Go, Orysia. I know you do not want to see this."

Priscilla's nails bit into her palms. How could he be so obtuse? Orysia's eyes were gleaming with fiendish anticipation. She would enjoy watching every minute of torture. When Orysia flung her arms around Lord Stenborough and kissed him, Priscilla wanted to gag. The two deserved each other, but not when Lady Stenborough was probably still lying on the floor in her own blood.

"Farewell, Lady Priscilla," crowed Orysia. "You should have listened when I warned you to watch out for danger."

"Is this how you make sure your predictions come true?" she retorted. "You warn someone of death and then inflict it yourself?"

"Mr. Harmsworth did not believe me." A satisfied smile spread across her lips. "He should have. Just like you should have." Her chortle remained behind as she strolled through a low door. The sound of her footfalls disappeared up stairs beyond it.

Priscilla strained to look past the edge of the rack. She was amazed to see Lady Stenborough on the rush-covered floor. Only the slow rise and fall of her back told Priscilla that the viscountess still lived.

Lord Stenborough's finger toyed with the pistol. She held her breath. His smile was too taut, his voice too high-pitched, his eyes shifting away too quickly. A single mistake could leave her dead before Lady Stenborough was.

"So quiet, Lady Priscilla? I thought you would have a dozen questions."

"It is obvious you are behind the murders here."

"Not me." He pointed the gun toward the door. "Orysia."

Priscilla knew he was not lying. Each time, Lord Stenborough had shown up too soon to be the attacker. His moaning and whining had provided a cover so no one noticed Orysia was absent. She had had time after talking to Priscilla and Neville yesterday to retrieve the crossbow. After the tournament, while Priscilla and Neville talked with the vicar and the children she had killed Mr. Harmsworth and then distracted them with her offer to read Priscilla's future. The supposed attack on her had been faked to focus suspicion elsewhere.

"It has been a successful plan," Lord Stenborough continued. "Orysia has played many roles in the theater, and if she had not been so careless, you would have been dead on the sea road, which would have kept everyone away from Stenborough Park long enough for my wife to die."

"That was Orysia tonight?" She had to keep him talking. He clearly had no interest in murdering anyone himself. A clever ploy, for if his plan had been discovered, he could have let Orysia hang alone.

"She has many skills. When Lady Stenborough is dead, they will think it is just another 'incident.'"

"All of this was to allow you to murder your wife?"

"Before she can divorce me."

"And take the remaining money in this estate?"

"Divorces are expensive, and Orysia is eager for the fine life I can give her once Rita is dead." He chuckled. "A simple plan, especially when the constable is convinced I am the victim. Think how much sympathy will be heaped on me when this last catastrophe—the loss of my dear wife—comes on my birthday. No one will suspect."

"Are you so sure of that?" She gritted her teeth as she pulled against the ropes. A low moan battered her lips. She was making her arms hurt worse.

He walked toward the door. "By the time you and Rita are discovered, you will both be dead. No one will think to look for you here. If they do, I shall share with the constable a few facts that will make him consider another suspect." His smile broadened. "After all, everyone is agog with the tale of your and Hathaway's brief betrothal."

"No one would believe Neville is behind these crimes!"

He walked back and kicked the lever at the top of the rack. When it turned, she shrieked. Darkness swelled to make his face waver. She battled to hold on to her senses. If she fainted, he would win. Blinking, she focused her eyes and clenched her numb fists. She gasped, the soft sound lost beneath his laughter. The ropes' tension had eased. Peering over her head, she saw the piece of wood that held the rollers in position had slipped out. If it was not pushed back into place, she might be able to free her arms. She must take care to time the attempt perfectly. Otherwise, Lord Stenborough would shoot her.

He went back to the door. Reaching to close it after himself, he said, "Farewell, Lady Priscilla."

He yelped and reeled back into the room, no longer holding the pistol. A man jumped into the dungeon and struck him again.

"Neville!" she cried.

He hit Lord Stenborough a third time, knocking

him to his knees. The candle flew from the viscount's hand and exploded in a pile of dry rushes.

Neville cursed and held out the pistol. "Get your wife, Stenborough!"

"No!"

The flames crackled as Priscilla struggled to free herself. The ropes still lashed her in place.

"Get her, Stenborough, or . . ." He did not need to finish his threat as he raised the gun.

Snarling an oath, the viscount stood and gathered up his wife.

Neville edged around him. He withdrew a knife from beneath his coat. Slicing awkwardly through the ropes holding her hands as he kept the gun pointed at the viscount, he asked, "Can you walk?"

"Yes. We need to leave!" She coughed as smoke swept over her as it had in the wagon. She remembered how Neville had told her that Orysia had been trying to put out the fire. It seemed likely the fortune-teller had *started* it.

She heard a thump and saw Lord Stenborough run out of the dungeon. Tossing the knife beside her, Neville leaped forward to keep him from closing the door. She started to climb down, but her legs were still bound. She gagged on the smoke while cutting through the ropes.

She crawled to where Lady Stenborough had been left by her husband. The barely conscious woman was moaning and choking on the smoke. Putting her hands under the viscountess's arms, she began to drag her toward the door. She could not see anything but flames, and she prayed she was going in the right direction.

Hands appeared out of the smoke. Lady Stenborough was lifted into waiting arms. An arm around

her waist guided her up the stairs as flames climbed
the rack to devour it. Men rushed in with buckets to
fight the fire.

"It is all right, Pris. You are safe."

Priscilla whirled to see Neville's pain-dimmed
smile. She started to embrace him, but drew back
when he swore and nearly fell.

She smiled as she steadied him so they could continue up the stairs and out into the foggy night.
"How did you keep Lord Stenborough from closing
the door?"

"I still have my good right jab," he said with a grin
as he struck the air. He wobbled, and she tightened
her grip on him.

"You are lucky you did not knock yourself out."

"I was lucky. One more blow sent Lord Stenborough scurrying away."

"Away? He got away?"

"Not far." He hooked a thumb toward where Constable Forshaw held a pistol to keep Lord
Stenborough *and* Orysia from fleeing. "They already
are blaming each other for the whole thing and
claiming innocence."

"Where did they take Lady Stenborough?"

"She has been taken to her rooms."

"How did you know where to look for me?"

He held up a clump of gold trim. "You left a trail
behind you. Stenborough was in too much of a
hurry to see his wife dead and Orysia in too much of
a hurry to get the viscountess's jewels to notice. I
found Forshaw, and we put together a very hasty
scheme that fortunately worked very well." He lifted
her arms to look at the welts on her wrists. "Damn
Stenborough!"

"I will have more respect for medieval martyrs now."

"This is my fault, Pris. I wanted to make certain the constable was in place before we came to your rescue. Then Orysia came out, and we had to subdue her. Stenborough had a gun, so I had to take care. If he had panicked, he could have killed you."

"But he did not." She shivered, although the night was warm. "I doubt he would have. He left the murders to Orysia."

He put his arm around her shoulders and turned her away from where the constable was interrogating his prisoners. She started to protest, then saw several men come to stand beside Constable Forshaw. Her dread that they were Stenborough's men faded when the viscount's shoulders drooped.

With the shout of "Mama!" her children came running toward her. Neville was included in the enthusiastic barrage of nearly strangling hugs. It took several moments for her to understand that Aunt Cordelia had insisted on returning to the house when she learned from Miss Young what had happened on the way to the pavilion.

"Is it true?" asked Isaac. "Is there really a dungeon here?"

Neville gently touched Priscilla's wrists and said, "Not any longer. What do you say, Pris, to a cup of something in your rooms?"

When she agreed, the children went ahead of them into the house. Aunt Cordelia followed at a more sedate pace, chiding them to go more slowly.

As she climbed the stairs with Neville, Priscilla said, "Next time you receive an invitation to a country house weekend, ask someone else to join you."

"Who else would I ask, Pris?" He paused one step

below her and wrapped his arms around her waist. Tilting her toward him, he whispered, "You are *my* lady fair."

She wanted to ask him if he was teasing or meant those words, but she had no chance as his mouth found hers for the slow, sensuous caress she had yearned to share with him. Later, she would ask him. Just now, she wanted to savor him holding her in his arms while she held him in her heart.

AUTHOR'S NOTE

Priscilla and Neville's adventures have just begun. Look for them again in October 2003 with their next story *The Greatest Possible Mischief*. Priscilla's daughter is about to be fired off into the Season, but a trip to Bath comes first. Neville never thought he'd be a chaperone at a party for youngsters, or that he'd be challenged to a duel by an old adversary. But the man is already dead when they get to the dueling green and Neville finds himself depending on Priscilla to prove he is innocent of murder. What is even more unbelievable: someone he never expected to have a crush on him may come between him and Priscilla. It would be much simpler if he could be honest about the real reason he came to Bath . . . but what if Priscilla says no?

Readers can contact me at:
P.O. Box 575
Rehoboth, MA 02769
Or visit my web site at:
www.joannferguson.com

Thrilling Romance from
Lisa Jackson